To Jona

Please Enjoy

Emma Richardson Dudney

Joey's Journey Home

by

Emma Richardson Dudney

1663 Liberty Drive, Suite 200
Bloomington, Indiana 47403
(800) 839-8640
www.AuthorHouse.com

This book is a work of fiction. People, places, events, and situations are the product of the author's imagination. Any resemblance to actual persons, living or dead, or historical events, is purely coincidental.

First published by AuthorHouse 02/16/05

ISBN: 1-4208-2704-9 (sc)
ISBN: 1-4208-2705-7 (dj)

Library of Congress Control Number: 2005900443

Printed in the United States of America
Bloomington, Indiana

This book is printed on acid-free paper.

Dedication

With love and gratitude to my husband, Lynn, who supported and encouraged me to complete the book and have it published, I dedicate this book to him and our children and grandchildren.

Our children never knew any of the hardships of "farm life." They were raised with modern bathrooms, telephones, electricity, and television. This book tells about another time and another life style. A time when children learned about farm animals first hand, how to milk a cow, how to gather eggs, how to work without pay, and how to live off the land. Entertainment was make believe, and learning to play without electronic games, or movies and cartoons. The book is fiction, but Gunsight, Texas is a very real place.

Chapter 1

Joey jerked awake and sat up in bed. "What was that noise?" He listened real close. "It sounds like a baby crying. Who is here with a baby?" he said to himself. He slipped out of bed and tiptoed to the bedroom door. Slowly he turned the door knob and peeked through the crack..... "It is a baby, but why is Mother holding it? Whose baby is it?"' His mind was racing with all kinds of thoughts and questions. About that time, Mrs. Stroud, a neighbor, came into the room and said, "Well, look who came to see his new baby sister." Sara, Joey's Mom, looked up and said, "Come on. It's all right. You can see her. Isn't she pretty, Joey?" Now this was all news to Joey. He was not too sure he even wanted a sister - much less one so little. Sara was holding her and singing to her and then Carl, Joey's Dad, said "We named her Beverly." Mother and Dad were smiling, and just looking at the new baby. Joey moved closer to get a better look. He shook his head and thought, "Who can remember a name like that?" Oh, well, he did not have anything to say to her anyway. There would be no reason for him to have to say Beverly.

The days passed so fast and then a year and then two years. Joey was getting taller. Bevi, as everyone called her, could talk now and was always bothering Joey. Joey thought it was fun - sometimes - to play with her and let her use him as her horse. Most of the time though, she just played with her doll and did dumb girl things.

Today was an extra special day. They were moving to a bigger farm. There was more land, better barns, and the house was bigger. Dad had promised Joey he could drive the wagon. Joey felt extra big. To drive the team of horses was really neat. He had driven them before, but not by himself. Today was different. It was just him and the horses and wagon. They were following Dad, who was pulling a trailer behind the truck. It took most of the day to get there and get the wagon and trailer unloaded. Then Joey and Dad put the horses in the corral fence and gave them feed and water. "You really did a good job driving the wagon," Dad said. " Did I?"asked Joey. "I like driving the horses. They are my favorite animal" replied Joey. Dad reached for Joey's hand and said, "Let's see if there is anything to eat. I bet Mom has it on the table by now." Sara and Carl talked about the good job Joey had done and how big he and Bevi were getting.

About a year after they had moved, Carl was listening to the news on a Sunday morning. The radio went silent. The battery was dead.

Carl told Sara and the children he was going into town. There had been something said about the United States being at war. He was gone most of the day. When Carl returned, he said, "The Japanese have bombed Pearl Harbor. We are really at war." Joey listened real close. He did not understand "war" or "bomb" or "Japanese." Just what was Japanese? Bevi knew not to ask questions. This was grown up talk. She edged closer to Joey and stayed just as close as she could.

Carl was sure he would have to join the army. He felt the time to leave would be very soon, and he wanted everything just right for Sara and the children. He wanted to move Sara and the children into town, but Sara would not budge. She had never lived in town and she was not about to start now. He sold some of the cows - keeping only a few for milk and butter. The horses were not sold - they had good blood lines and Carl wanted to be sure he had a good horse when he returned home to the farm. Sara wanted to keep the chickens.

Then the day arrived for Carl to report for duty in the army. Joey tried hard to be big and not cry, but Sara was crying and the tears just seemed to roll down and he couldn't stop them. Carl put his arms around Joey and Bevi, and hugged them close. "Now, Joey, you've got to help Mom take care of the farm. Promise me you will not be a problem and will do just what she says," Carl said. "I won't be gone very long and I need you to be strong and help out here."

With tears streaming down their cheeks, both children promised to be good and to help on the farm.

It was lonesome with Carl gone. Sara worked hard to keep everything just as he would have. After the children were in bed at night, she would set down and write to Carl. She told him everything the children did, just how grown up Joey was, about the farm animals, how many eggs she gathered, how much she loved him and how she longed for him to return. She wrote every night. She did not want a mail call for Carl's unit to happen and him to not have a letter. This was really important to her. There were letters that came from Carl, and Sara would read them to the children. The weeks turned into months and then a year, then two years. Joey and Bevi were growing so fast, and there were so many things on the farm to be taken care of. Sara tried to keep the children busy and happy.

Chapter 2

Joey and Bevi loved to play army and cowboys and Indians in the bottom pasture. There was a large pipe line running across the pasture, and the ground was sandy and warm and it was so much fun to walk the pipe. Bevi could do it just as good as Joey, except for one thing - Joey could run on the pipe and Bevi couldn't. She tried and tried, but always fell off.

One warm day, the children were playing cowboys and Indians and Bevi saw something move over behind the trees. She stood very still. Joey was at the other end and came running, "What are you looking at?" Bevi pointed to the trees and said, "Something moved over there. See, it moved again." Joey was surprised to see a black pickup behind the tree. "Let's go see who it is," he said. Off they ran, but before they got very close, Joey stopped and said, "let's be quite. Play like we are watching Indians." "Okay," said Bevie. They ran down in the ditch and crawled up under some brush. They got as close as they could and stayed out of sight. There were two men, and they had on big hats and black pants and boots. "Look," whispered Bevi, "they have Mr. Brown's cow in the pickup." "Shh," Joey said, "I don't want them to hear us." The men loaded another cow into the pickup and closed the sideboard gate. Then one of the men cut a limb from a small mesquite bush and drug it on the ground. He was wearing a brown hat and a red shirt. The other man got into the pickup and started to drive with the man in the brown hat riding on the back, dragging the tree limb behind the pickup. Joey and Bevi watched until the pickup was out of sight. "I guess Mr. Brown sold them some of his cows," said Joey. "Yah," said Bevie, "I guess he did."

Saturday was the day Sara and the children went into town to sell the eggs and butter. Today she wanted to buy the children some new shoes. With money Sara had saved, and the sale of the butter and eggs, just maybe she would have enough to get everything they needed. Joey especially liked to go into town. He could stand around the Court House Square where all the farmers and ranchers gathered and listen to the men talk. He missed his Dad so much. Sara always parked close so he could do that while she did all the other things that had to be done.

After their trip to town, Sara asked the children to help her look for the cows in the pasture. They hurried off to find the cows and sure enough there they were standing in the shade of a tree by the tank.

There were four of them. Two were brown and white and the other two were kinda white with a lot of black spots and there was one baby calf. There would soon be two more.

The next day being Sunday; Sara and the children were ready for Church. This was the Sunday the Preacher would be there. Since he had to take care of several small churches, he only came one Sunday a month. After church, everyone stood around and talked and visited. Bevi liked to play with the other kids and Joey liked to listen to the men talk. This was a fun time.

Sara called the children to get in the car. As she helped Bevi into the car, she turned to Tom Brown, a neighbor, and said "I checked on my cows and they were all there yesterday." "That's good," Tom said, "I'm looking in all the pastures around. I can't find all of mine yet." Bevie popped up and said, "I saw the cow you sold in the shiny pickup." Sara jerked her head around and said, "Bevi, you know that's not true. It is very ugly to say things that are not true." "But it is," Bevi said, "Didn't we Joey? Didn't we see the red cow in the shiny pickup?" "Yah, we did" said Joey. "The men loaded her up and that other little red cow too." "When did you see this Joey?" asked Tom. "Oh, it was three days ago when me and Bevie were playing," Joey said. Sara could not believe what she was hearing. She did not remember seeing anything. "Where - just where did you see this?" she snapped. Now Bevi wanted to be just as important as Joey, so she said "I seed it behind the trees when me and Joey was playing on the pipe. We ran and watched them put the cow in the pickup and sweep the ground too." "Sweep the ground?" Sara said. "What do you mean - sweep the ground?" "They did," Bevi said. "That man in the brown hat cut a tree and swept the ground."

Tom and his wife Kate were surprised to hear the children. Tom scratched his head and said, "Sara would it be all right if Kate and I come over and let Joey and Bevi show us where they saw all of this?" Sara was glad for them to come. She just wanted to be sure the children were not making up this story. She really questioned them hard on the way home. Joey did not have much to say, but he did say everything Bevi said was true. The man had really swept the ground.

Sara was surprised they had not mentioned it to her. "Joey, why didn't you tell me this?" she asked. "Oh, I don't know, I heard some men talking when we were in town about selling cows. And Mr. Tom had said awhile back he needed to sell some."

Tom, Kate and Sara followed as the children ran to the bottom pasture. When they got to the pipe, Tom asked if this was where the children were playing. Bevi said, "I can show you where I was when I saw the pickup. It scared me, cause it moved and I didn't know what it was." She ran down and stood next to the turn-off valve on the pipe line. "I was right here, and I saw through the trees right over there." she said as she pointed to a clump of mesquite trees. Joey agreed with her and said, "We ran down into the ditch and over there behind those trees. You can see where they were from there." "Did you crawl over the fence?" asked Sara. "No ma'am" said Joey. "We could see them from our side."

Kate took Bevi's hand and said, "Bevi, honey, can you show me right where you were." Joey and Bevi took them to the spot where they stood, and sure enough, they could see the children's foot prints in the sand next to the trees. "Joey," Tom said, "could you walk with me over there and show me exactly where the pickup was?" "Yes sir," said Joey. "I sure can. I think I can show you where they cut the trees, too." Sara, Kate and Bevi walked to the fence with Tom and Joey and waited while they crossed over the fence and looked around on Tom's property.. When they came back, Tom said, "Well, Bevi, you were sure right. They did sweep the ground. I wonder Sara, if you would mind if I have Sheriff Sam Norris come out to talk with the children?" "What else could they possibly tell?" she asked. "I'm not sure they would be of any more help," Tom said. "But Sheriff Sam might think of a question to ask that I haven't, and he does need to hear first hand from the children."

Chapter 3

Sheriff Sam Norris parked the car and waited for Joey, Sara and Bevi. He could see them coming up the path from the barn. "Sam," said Sara, "it has been a long time since I saw you. What brings you out this way?" Then Sara remembered what Tom had said. "Open the gate, Bevi. Come in Sam. You remember the children. Don't you? This is Joey and Bevi." said Sara. Sam held out his hand to Joey and said, "I'm Sam Norris, the Sheriff of the county and a good friend of your Mom and Dad." He turned and picked up Bevi and said "And this must be Bevi. My, my what a big pretty girl you are." Sam had known Carl and Sara before they married. He was elected Sheriff just before the war. Sam was a big man, over 6 ft. tall and weighed over 200 lbs. To Bevi, he looked kinda like the giant, Goliath, in the story her dad had read to her from the Bible.

In the kitchen, Sara poured the milk up into the large jars, and placed it in the refrigerator. Then she asked Sam if he would like a cup of coffee. As Sara was making the coffee, Joey and Bevi counted the eggs and placed them in the cartons. Sara poured milk for Joey and Bevi and coffee for Sam and herself. As she sat down at the table, she said "what brings you out this way? I'm sure it's not just for a visit?" "No," he said, "it's not. I talked with Tom Brown, and he reported a couple of his Hereford cows missing. I was over there today and we went down into the pasture where the pickup was. Tom and Kate told me that Joey and Bevi saw the men load the cows up. I just wanted to talk to them a little and see if they could remember what the men looked like." Sara was sure the children had already told everything they knew, but she did not object to Sam asking them questions.

"Joey, are you sure you saw the men load up two cows?" Sam asked. "Yes sir, we did" he replied. "Did the men know you saw them." "Oh, no, I don't think so," said Joey. "They sure never looked at us," Bevi put in. "I think we were hid pretty good, and Joey wouldn't let me talk either." Sam sipped on his coffee, and took out a pad and pen and wrote down some things and then he looked at Bevi and said, "Do you know who the men were?" "No sir," replied Bevi, "I couldn't see their faces."

Sam then asked the children about the pickup. Joey said it was just a pickup - black and kinda new looking. Sam waited for them to remember more. Finally, Bevi said, "It had a board fence on it." Joey shook his head and said, "Girls!, of course, it did. But that's called sideboards. You are so dumb." "I am not dumb - and sides - I saw it first.." "Now, now , Joey, Bevi," said Sara, "let's not be ugly. Sam is here on business and does not want to hear you fuss."

Sam was amused at Bevi's spunk. She seemed to know what she saw alright. "Well now, Bevi" Sam said, "can you tell me anything about that board fence? What color it was or how many boards it had or just anything you remember would help me a lot." Well, that made Bevi feel better. She thought about it and tried to remember just what color it was. "I'm not sure what color it was" she said. "I don't think Joey has a color like that. But I think it was a reddish brown gray, and it had four boards on it." Sam smiled. He was not real sure he had ever seen a color like that before. He wrote it down in his little pad, and then he turned to Joey. "Can you add anything to that, Joey?" he asked. "No sir, just it was not really all painted, it was like different faded colors showing through, sorta."

Sam finished his coffee and picked up his hat to go. "I think maybe the children have added some to the description of the pickup. We should be able to spot it if it ever shows back up around here."

Sara was a little troubled. "Sam, do you think we are in any danger? Maybe I should have moved to town like Carl wanted us to." "Oh, now Sara, don't get to thinking like that," Sam said. "Everything will be all right; I will keep an eye out for you and so will Tom and Kate." As the car was leaving, Bevi waved, and hugged Rags the dog.

"Well," said Sara, "would you like for me to read to you after we eat?" Both children were excited and said yes. They hurried and as soon as the dishes were put away, Sara reached up on the top shelf and showed them the new book. "Oh, boy," said Joey, "Miss Smith, my teacher, said this is really a good book." "What is it" asked Bevi. "*Lassie, Come Home*." " It's about a boy and his dog," Sara said. She read for a long time. She noticed Bevi getting sleepy, and Joey was not far behind. She stopped at the end of the chapter and promised to read more tomorrow night.

After the children were in bed, she warmed the left over coffee, and got out pen and paper to write to Carl. It was a hard decision, but she did not tell him about Tom's cows being stolen. Neither did she tell about the children seeing the men in the pasture. Carl did not need this worry while he was away.

Just as she finished her letter, she heard Rags, their dog, growl. He always stayed on the porch at night. It was unusual for him to growl at anyone he knew, but then, she had not heard a car drive up. Sara went to the door to see what was bothering the dog. He was not on the porch. "He's probable just chasing a rabbit or some other creature" she said to herself. She turned the light out and went to bed.

Chapter 4

The next morning as Sara started to the barn to milk the cow, she wondered where Rags was. Maybe he was at the barn. But still, it was strange for him to not be there at the door when she stepped out. As she opened the gate, there was a cigar butt on the ground. It had not been there the night before, but then maybe Sam had thrown it down, but no, she didn't see Sam smoke while he was there.

After the milking was finished, she opened the chicken house and let the chickens out, put water out for them and headed back to the house. The children would be awake by now, and she had to hurry to get Joey off to catch the school bus.

When she got to the gate, she saw the cigar butt again, and reached down and picked it up. She wondered just who had dropped it. Entering the house, she called to the children to come to the kitchen and eat. "Better hurry Joey. It's nearly time for the bus." Sara fixed cereal and milk, put it on the table and went to rush them up some. She was shocked to find Joey's bed empty. Bevi was sitting on her bed rubbing her eyes. "Where's Joey?" Sara asked. "I don't know. I been sleeping," Bevi said. Sara grabbed Bevi up in her arms, and ran to the kitchen. She sat Bevi down to eat her cereal and ran outside and called "Joey!, Joey!" as loud as she could. There was no answer.

Sara was beginning to get scared. What to do now? Where could he be? Why did he leave? How did he leave the house and she did not hear him? All of these questions were running through her mind. She hurried back into the house and searched Joey's room again. His clothes and shoes were missing. There was just one thing to do now - she would go back to the barn, maybe he was there. In her mind, she was thinking he might be playing a trick on her. He did like to hide and play games.

She picked up Bevi and headed for the bedroom to get some clothes on her. About that time she heard the door open and Joey call, "Mom?" "Where have you been?" Sara demanded. Without giving him time to answer she said, "Don't you ever leave this house again without telling me. Where have you been?" "Well," he stammered, "I, ah, I woke up during the night and I heard Rags barking at the barn and it was a different kind of bark. I thought about our new calf, and I was scared someone might try to steal it like they did Mr. Brown's, so I dressed and went to see why Rags was barking."

Sara was mad, glad, and shocked at her son. What could he be thinking? "Well?" snapped Sara. "What was he barking at?" "I don't know for sure, Mom, but I really think someone was at the barn." "What!" She said. "You think someone was at our barn?" "Yes ma'am, I do." Joey was trying to be as grown up as he knew how, and yet he knew mom was really mad at him. "When I got down there by the hay stack, I thought I heard a voice and Rags cried out like he was hurt and came running to me. I was scared, so I grabbed him and crawled into the hole in the hay where we play sometimes. Me and Rags just laid real still and then Rags started that deep growl he does sometimes and crawled out in front of me. I could hear something but I was too scared to move. I was there a long time before Rags came back. I guess we just went to sleep and stayed there the rest of the night."

Sara was so glad he was alright. She really forgot to be mad at him any more. But for someone to be at the barn - now that was another matter. Maybe they were in danger. Tom Brown needed to know about this.

"Well," Sara said, "you better hurry and eat. You will need some clean clothes on before school. Hurry now, and don't you tell anyone about this at school, do you hear?" She helped him change for school, and comb his hair. He had to run to get to the bus stop. Sara stood on the porch and watched as the bus pull up and stop, then leave. With a sigh of relief, she went back into the house with Bevi.

As soon as Sara cleaned the kitchen and helped Bevi get dressed, she headed for Tom and Kate's house. They were surprised to see her. "What brings you two over this morning?" asked Tom. "Well," she said, "there was some excitement at our place and I just wanted to talk to you some." After she had told them everything, Tom asked all kinds of questions. "Sara, I'm not sure what to make of this, but I do feel we need to let Sam know about this. I'm going to go look around your barns. Maybe I will see something that will give us a clue about what or who was there."

Tom walked all around the barn, and checked all the cribs in both sheds. On his way back to the house, he stopped and picked up something and came on to the house. Sara was nervous and a little jumpy. She was glad Kate was there with her. When Tom came in, he sat down and put a cigar butt on the table. "Who has been here that smokes cigars?" he asked. "No one that I know of," said Sara, and she went to the shelf in the pantry and brought back the one she had picked up that morning at the gate. "Look at this. It was at the gate this morning. I just thought maybe Sam threw it down last night when he was here." "Sam came by last night?" Tom asked. "Yes, he said he had been over to your place and he just wanted to talk with the children some." Sara said. "Sam didn't go to the barn last night. That cigar couldn't be his" she said. "That means someone was here after Sam left, and Rags did bark and growl at something. I just thought it was probably some wild animal."

"Was Joey and Bevi able to tell him anymore?" "Not much, Bevi remembered the pickup had sideboards on it is about all." Tom shook his head and picked up both cigar butts. "I'm going to go see Sam. There are some footprints at the barn, and Rags is not getting around too good. Someone may have given him a pretty good kick." Sara had not noticed the dog. He had been laying on the porch as they left to go to Tom and Kate's house. She did not recall seeing him walk around any.

Tom found Sam at the courthouse. He waited until Ted White, a friend and neighbor, left and then he went into Sam's office. Sam was surprised to see him so soon after his visit the day before. "What brings you in today, Tom?" he asked. "Well, Sam, we may have a little problem. I'm not sure, I just wanted you to hear about this as soon as possible." "What is it?" Sam asked. Tom told Sam everything that Sara had told him that morning. "Footprints, you say?" Sam mused. "Were they real sharp, fresh prints?" "Gosh, Sam," Tom said, scratching his head, "they looked pretty fresh to me, and Sara said no one had been there except you." "Did they look like that print we found down in your pasture?" asked Sam. "Well, now that you mention it, maybe, just maybe. It is a big print alright." Tom replied.

Sam reached for the top drawer of the file cabinet, and pulled out a file. “While I have you here, I forgot to ask about your cows. Did you have your brand on them?” Sam asked. “No,” Tom said, “I just didn’t want to mess up the hide with a brand mark...but I’ll tell you what I did. I took my punch and put 3 holes in their left ear, shaped like a triangle.” “Great,” said Sam. “I will add that to the official record here. That will make it official now when we find them.” “Is Sara at home now?” asked Sam. “Yeah. She is a little nervous and jumpy though.” Tom said. Tom turned to leave, then he remembered the cigars. “By the way Sam, I found this down by Sara’s barn and she found this one at the gate to the yard this morning. She thought you might have thrown it down as you were leaving.” Sam looked at the cigar butts. They were not a cheap cigar. “I don’t smoke,” he said. “I didn’t think so” said Tom. “Two cigar butts could mean there were two people there last night” Sam said. “It takes awhile to smoke a cigar.”

Sam went over the information Tom had given him and decided it was time for him to look around some more. He went to the supply room and brought back the plaster he used to lift prints with. On his way out the door, he noticed it was looking like rain. He wanted to lift that boot print before it rained, if possible.

Sara saw Sam coming down the lane. She was so glad to see him. Bevi was on the porch and she waved to him as he got out of the car. “Joey slept in the hay last night,” she said. “That’s what I heard,”

Sam called back. "Is your Mom here?" "I'm here Sam. It is sure good to see you," Sara said. "I'm going down to the barn and look around some. I want to lift the boot print if I can. Why don't you make some coffee while I do that?" Sara was glad to do just that. She had just put bread aside to rise, and needed a cup herself. Bevi could have some juice with them.

Sam moved around the barn very carefully. He did not want to disturb any prints. There, that looked like the one Tom told him about. Boy, that was a big print. He mixed the plaster and poured it over the print. Now he had to wait for it to set. While he waited, he walked around and checked the cribs in the barn and then over to the haystack. Sure enough, there was Joey's prints where he had crawled into the hay stack. As he turned to go back to check the plaster, he noticed something caught on the limb next to the hay stack. He reached for the limb, and looked closer, funny, that looked like a feather, maybe from a hat band. Not any birds around that he had seen with orange feathers. He very carefully removed the feather, and placed it in a bag. It might be evidence, he wanted to gather everything he could find. There were some other marking in the dirt, but nothing real clear. He needed to check the plaster before it started to rain.

The plaster was ready and he lifted it up, and sure enough, there was the print. It was really pretty good. Sam was pretty proud of himself. He had not lifted many prints, and this one was really good.

He returned to the house and had coffee with Bevi and Sara. Bevi was a real motor mouth today.

Joey had two more weeks of school, then the whole summer. He could hardly wait. Sara had scolded him pretty good for sleeping in the hay. It wasn't that bad. He wasn't scared as long as Rags was there. Anyway, he had promised not to do that again.

Sam had been out and Tom had been over, but there had not been any word on Tom's stolen cows. Joey was standing looking through the fence at the new calves when Sara walked up. "Aren't they something else?" she said. "They sure are," Joey answered. "Mom, do we have to burn their side like the other cows? I just know it hurts, and they are so small." Sara was not sure how she could manage to brand the calves without Carl. She had intended to talk to Tom and see what he thought. She didn't want it to be easy for anyone to steal the calves, but neither did she want people feeling sorry for her and doing things for free. "I don't know, Joey. Why don't we talk to Tom and see if there is another way? What do you think of that?" she said. "That's okay by me." Joey replied.

Sara had finished the "Lassie" book and taken it back to the library. The children really enjoyed it. She found another one she was sure they would like. It was about a horse called Black Beauty. She would start it tonight. It took her mind off all the other problems.

Chapter 5

With school out now, Joey was a big help to Sara. They had some new chickens, and another calf was on the way. Tom had put some holes in the right ear of the other calves. He made a square with a hole in the middle. Joey was happy with that. Tom told him to be sure and not tell anyone about the holes. That will be our way of proving the animal is yours if it is ever stolen. Joey wanted to do that to all the cows, but Tom told him the ones with the brand was safe enough. Just the new ones was all that really needed it.

It was early June and Sara was canning the garden vegetables. She was remembering the days when Carl was home. It had been over three years since he left. It would sure be good to have him home again.

"Joey, why don't you take a break and check the cows. I don't want that new calf to come and us not know it." Sara said. Joey was glad to do that. He did not like to shell peas. Bevi wanted to go with him, but Sara said she had to stay at the house. Bevi stuck her lip out and pouted at this, but it didn't take long for her to find something new to talk about.

Now Joey really liked the outdoors. He and Rags could walk the pasture for hours. "Come on, Rags," he called as he ran out the gate. Rags came running and off they went. It was such a beautiful day, and there was not a breeze anywhere. As they ran down the path into the bottom pasture, a rabbit ran in front of them. Now, the only thing Rags liked better than being with Joey was chasing rabbits. Off the rabbit ran with Rags right behind him. Joey knew it would be a while before Rags came back.

He checked the bottom tank, and there were only two cows there. As he rounded the trees on the south side of the tank, he thought he heard something, but did not see anything. He ran through the sand to the pipe line and jumped up on it. As he was running down the pipe, he saw a flash off to his left, and heard something - like a door slam. He jumped off the pipe and started for the ditch and the trees. Just as he reached the trees, he saw the truck and trailer just inside their property. Joey remembered what Sheriff Sam had said. He needed a better description of the men and pickup. This looked like the same men that took Mr. Tom's cows. He had to be quiet, and stay out of sight. He crawled farther into the brush and found a hole to peek through. He watched as they loaded up Mom's three heifers, the ones without brands and then they took Old Bessie. The cow that was expecting a new calf just any time. They put the cow in the back of the pickup and the three heifers in the trailer.

The man that seemed like the boss, called to the other man. "Jake, check around and make sure we are the only ones here. You might check that tank up there. I thought there was another calf the last time." "Okay," said Jake, and off he went.

Joey was real still. He did not want them to know he was there. After a few minutes, he thought about the license number on the pickup. He scooted a little to his right, he could see it really good. He took a stick and was about to scratch the number in the dirt when suddenly, he was grabbed and jerked up.

"Well, what do we have here?" Jake said. Before Joey could look around, Jake put his hand over Joey's eyes and mouth. "Hey, Bob, look what I found spying on us." He carried Joey on his hip and when he got to the pickup, he dropped him on the ground. "Stay put Boy. Just what do you think you're doing anyway?" Jake said. Joey was so scared he was shaking. He was afraid to speak, he thought he might just cry and that was not what a man did. He ducked his head and didn't say anything.

“What do we do with this?” Jake asked. “Well now,” said Bob, “Where did you find him?” “I followed his tracks from the pipe over to that crop of trees there.” said Jake. Bob shook his head and looked around. “Are you sure he’s by himself or is someone else out there? We sure can’t leave him here, especially since he was spying on us,”Bob said. “He’s all I saw.” replied Jake. He turned to Joey and said “Was anyone with you Boy?” Joey still couldn’t make his mouth work. He just shook his head. “We’ll just have to take him with us a ways” said Bob. “I need to see what the Boss will say.”

They tied a rag around Joey’s mouth and tied his hands behind his back. Jake took a sack out of the truck and put it over Joey’s head, and pulled it down around his body. Then they took a rope and pulled it really tight around his waist and legs. One of them picked him up, and put him in the pickup. After a few minutes, and the men closing the doors, Boom! Boom! Joey jumped and listened real hard. He could not figure out what it was. It really sounded like a gunshot, but he was not sure. He was so scared. He was shaking all over. He heard the pickup door open and close again. When the pickup moved, he nearly fell. He leaned against the sideboards, and tried to move to the front of the pickup bed. He inched along, and finally got to the corner. He eased down as best he could, but the rope was so tight it was hurting some and it was really hard to breath with this rag tied around his mouth. He leaned his head over and touched Old Bessie. He tried to talk to her but could not get any words out, since they had tied rag around his mouth.

Chapter 6

Sara looked out the door. Joey should be in soon. He had been gone nearly three hours. Oh, well, maybe he was just loafing with Rags. After all, boys had to do that sometimes. She had finished the canning, milked the cow, fed the chickens, and gathered the eggs. She poured the milk into the jars and placed it in the refrigerator. Now, she was a little upset. Just where was Joey? She stepped out on the porch. "Joey, Joey, where are you? It's time to come in," she called. There was no answer. She waited a while longer and called again. Still no answer. It was nearly dark by now. She decided maybe Joey had seen Tom and gone over to his place. She and Bevi would drive over and pick him up.

As Sara drove up, Kate called out, "Come on over, we were just having some lemonade." Sara got out and Bevi ran to the porch. "Where's Joey?" asked Tom. "Is he not here with you?" asked Sara. "No," Tom answered, "we haven't seen him. Did you send him over?" Sara looked around, eased down into a chair and tried to think where he could be. "No, I didn't," she said. Then she told them about sending him to look for the cows, and how she had called and called for him.

Tom picked up his hat and said, "Kate, you and Bevi go get Sam. I'm going to go back with Sara and look around that bottom pasture some before it gets too dark." He got his big flashlight and took Sara by the arm. "Want me to drive?" he said. She just nodded her head. The tears started falling and just would not stop.

Tom and Sara ran to the bottom pasture calling for Joey and then they would whistle for Rags. There was not a sound. After a while, they heard a horn blowing at the house. Tom knew that would be Sam or Kate. He was hoping Joey would be there too. He and Sara started for the house in a run.

When they reached the house, there were lights everywhere. Sara was so scared she could not stop shaking. What could have happened to Joey? Tom told Sam where they had been and how long they had been down there. "Did you see any cows?" Sam asked. "Come to think of it, no, we did not. I was just thinking of Joey." Tom said.

Sam sat down at the table and pulled out a large piece of paper. "We need to draw a rough picture of the property. Also, Tom, I need to know if any fences have been cut." Tom and Sara helped with the drawing, and then Sam said, "It's just too dark to see anything tonight. Sara, I don't believe Joey is in the pasture. He would have answered you and Tom....and I think Rags would have come to you if they were there."

Tears came to Sara's eyes again, and a million thoughts and questions ran through her mind. Just why had she sent him to do a man's job? The deputy that had come out with Sam said, "I think I need to take a light and check around all the tanks, just in case he might be in trouble there." "That's a good idea, Dan," said Sam. "My big light is on the porch."

They waited a long time. The men were making plans for the morning when Dan stepped up on the porch. Sara ran to the door. He was holding Rags in his arms. She gasped and took the dog in her arms and began to cry again. He had been shot in the head. Dan looked at the drawing again, and showed them where he had found Rags. He said, " the fence has been cut and there are tire tracks. It's too dark to tell much tonight."

Tom stood looking at the map for a long time at the spot where Rags had been. "Sam, I have a hunch Joey came upon those rustlers again." "I do, too," said Sam. "I just can't figure out why they would take Joey though and kill Rags. It just doesn't make any sense." said Dan. "We need to search the pastures in the morning. Joey could be tied up out there somewhere. We don't know that they took him. It just looks that way."

Chapter 7

The pickup went pretty fast for a long time. Joey could tell by the lights flashing through the sack, that it was dark. He wondered just where he was. He had worked his way to the corner. He tried to imagine just what direction they were going. There had been so many turns, and the sun was not shining and he just could not figure what direction they were traveling. The pickup finally slowed down, and pulled off the road. Joey heard the men get out. They were talking, but he couldn't understand what they were saying.

As soon as their steps faded, Joey got busy trying to slip his hands and arms loose. He twisted and twisted, finally one hand slipped out. He jerked and jerked. First to the left then the right, finally, the rope on the sack slipped. He had to work fast. He did not know just where the men had gone. He eased the sack off his head and took the rag off from around his mouth. It sure had a bad taste to it.

He petted Old Bessie, the cow, and moved so he could see around some more. There was a cafe and he could see four people in it and there was a lady behind the counter. He studied the situation for a few minutes and decided he could crawl over the sideboards on the far side. As soon as the car that was coming passed, he was over the side before you could blink. He ran just as hard as he could and ducked into the ditch when he saw a car light coming. He wanted to get as far away from those men as he could. He would run and then hit the ditch and lay on his belly until the car lights passed. He did this several times. One time he looked around and thought he saw the pickup pull onto the highway. He darted into the ditch, and started looking for a good place to hide. He found a culvert running under the highway. It didn't take him long to crawl into it. He waited to hear the pickup pass. "There, I hear it now," he softly said to himself. It passed over him very slowly. He lay in the culvert for a long time.

When he crawled out, there wasn't a light in sight. With a deep sigh, he said, "Now, which way to go. How am I going to find my way home?" He knew by now, Mom was really worried about him. Maybe he should go down the next lane and see if he could find someone to help him. If he could just find a house, surely someone could tell him how to get home. But what if those men lived around here? What if it was their house down the next lane? He wanted to go home, but he didn't know where home was.

He started walking slowly down the highway, being very careful to watch for cars. There's a mailbox . It just might belong to someone down the lane to the right. He looked as hard as he could, but it was just too dark to see much. Joey was thinking hard. What was it Dad had told him just before he went to war? "When you think you're right, it's all right to do it? Is that what he said?" Joey remembered he had said, "Just trust in the Lord - He will never fail you." Well, Joey was sure at a spot to have to trust someone. The longer he thought about it, the more positive he was that he really needed some help. He was going down this lane and ask for help!

He started down the lane and had walked for several minutes before he heard a dog bark. "Oh, my, I hope he knows I'm not a prowler, and that I just need some help." he said to himself. When Joey located the dog by the sound of his bark, sure enough there was a light behind those trees. He hurried down the lane, and the dog came running toward him barking up a storm. "Nice doggie, I ain't going to hurt you. I just need some help." Joey stood very still and let the dog smell him. He kept talking to the dog in a real soft voice, just the way Dad had done when other animals or dogs came to the house. He wanted the dog to like him. Finally the dog licked his hand.. "Good dog," he said. They started walking on toward the house. Then Joey saw a man standing on the porch. "Who's there?" he called. "It's just me sir, Joey Thomas. I need some help". "Well, come on in the yard so I can see you," the man said. Joey hurried into the yard. As he stepped up on the porch, a woman came to the door. "Who's here Dave?" she asked. "I'm just about to find out." he said. Joey held out his hand, "I'm Joseph William Thomas, but everyone calls me Joey, sir." "Well now, my name is Dave Gray and this here is my wife Fran. What seems to be your trouble, young man?" "Why, Dave," said Fran, "this is just a boy. Where are your manners? Come on in the house. Where do you live Joey?" she said. "Well, me and my mom and sister live in Gunsight. A little ways out of Breckenridge," Joey said. They were in the house now and something sure smelled good. It smelled like fried chicken. Joey's mouth began to water, he could nearly taste that chicken

Dave started to sit down, but Fran said "Is that blood on your hands? Are you hurt? Let me look at that. Dave, this boy has scratches all over his arms and hands." Joey was trying to answer the questions, but there were just too many. Dave looked at him and said, "You want to tell me what the trouble is son?" "Where's your dad?" "I don't rightly know, sir, he's at war somewhere." "You mean he is in the service, and you and your Mom and sister are on the farm all by yourself?" asked Fran. "Yes ma'am, that's where we are."

Dave was wondering just how this boy got so far from home. It would be close to eighty miles he guessed. "Is your Mom stranded in the car with a flat or something?" he asked. "Oh, no sir, I got stole with the calves and Ole Bessie, and I finally got the sack off my head and crawled out when they stopped to eat, and I ran as hard as I could... and" "Whoa, there," said Dave, "You were what....stole?" "Yes sir.

You see I was just checking on the cows and..." Fran came and sat down by him and said "Dave this child is scared. You need to go get the Sheriff or someone." "Do you know Sheriff Norris?" Joey asked. "No," said Dave. "Our Sheriff's name is Fleming." "Now, slow down Joey, and tell me again about checking on the cows," said Dave. "Well sir, I was checking on the cows and I got stole and put in the pickup with Old Bessie, and..." "Son, are you trying to tell me that you were kidnapped when someone stole some calves?" asked Dave. Joey had not heard the word "kidnapped" before. "Well, sir, if that word means stole, yes, sir, that's what happened." Dave looked at Fran and said, "I think you're right. I'm going to go get the Sheriff and let him hear this story." He reached for his hat. "I'll be back just as quick as I can," he called as he went out the door.

Fran sat some cold chicken on the table for Joey. Nothing had ever tasted so good. He drank two glasses of milk and ate three pieces of chicken. "Would you let me clean those scratches on your arms and face? And maybe you would like to lie down until Dave gets back?" Fran asked. She could tell by his eyes he was scared and tired. "Yes, ma'am, that would be okay." It seemed like a long time had passed to Joey. He was wondering just where the Sheriff was. He leaned his head over on the arm of the couch and in just a few minutes had drifted off to sleep. He kept saying something but Fran could not make out what it was. Poor child, he looked so young. Fran could hardly keep the tears from falling.

Chapter 8

Dave drove faster than he had ever driven. "This is one of those times when I wish we had one of those telephones." he thought to himself. When he reached town, he turned down Main Street and headed for the courthouse. Jim Fleming, the Sheriff, usually stayed at the courthouse during the week. Dave parked and ran up the steps, then down the narrow hall that led to the Sheriff's Office. The lights were on, so Dave knew he had to be here. Dave knocked on the door but no one came. He listened and he could hear someone talking. He banged again real hard on the door and called, "Jim, Jim, come on out here. I got a real problem." In just a minute or two, the door opened and the Sheriff stepped out. "What's the problem Dave?" he asked. Dave was excited and talking louder than usual. "Jim, you won't believe this, but there is a young kid and I mean young, I bet he's no more than ten or eleven years old, came up to our house a bit ago and said he had been kidnapped when some calves were stolen. This kid lives in Gunsight, a small community south of Breckenridge, and Jim that's right at eighty miles away - or maybe farther!" Jim looked around and didn't see anyone. "Where is he?" "Out at the house. Fran was feeding him when I left." Jim scratched his head, turned back into his office and picked up his hat and gun. "Well, let's go. I need to hear this story. I'll just follow you Dave." They circled the courthouse and was back on the road.

Dave and Jim parked out front and went into the house at once. "Where's the boy?" asked Dave. "He's over there on the couch. He is really having some bad dreams I think. He keeps talking in his sleep, but I can't tell what he is saying." Fran said. "Well, Jim here needs to talk with him some." Fran went to wake him up. When she touched his arm, he sat straight up. "It's alright, Joey. Dave is back with the Sheriff and they would like for you to tell them what happened."

Joey was scared and he tried really hard to tell the Sheriff just what happened. This Sheriff didn't seem to like him much. He never wrote down anything. "Did you know the men that took you?" Jim asked. "No, sir, I didn't. They tied me up and put a sack over my head and I couldn't see their faces." "Are you sure this is the truth? Did someone really kidnap you, or did you just run away from home?" the Sheriff asked. "Your story sure doesn't make much sense." Joey looked right at the Sheriff and said "No, sir, I sure never ran away and I'm not telling no story either. My Mom would tan my back side if I did that."

"I've got to do some checking on this" said Jim Fleming. "I don't know just what to think. This story sure sounds made up." He ran his hand through his hair, and toyed with his hat and then he said, "I'll be back in touch tomorrow, that is, if the boy can stay with you tonight." "That's not a problem." said Dave. "He will be just fine here. I doubt Fran would let you take him tonight anyway." Fran was concerned. She noticed he had not asked many questions and had not written down anything. He had not asked his parents names, or how to get in touch with them. How could he check things out and not have that information? It really seemed strange that the Sheriff would just assume the boy was not telling the truth. She was sure the boy was being very honest. He was so young and so scared.

Jim Fleming didn't waste any time getting back to town. Just as soon as he got to the office, he got on the two way radio and said, "2-K-B, this is 1-J, do you copy? " there was no reply. "2-K-B, this is 1-J, we got problems. Come in" "2-K-B here," came the reply. "Go to the barns. I'll see you in half an hour." Jim needed to find out just what had happened. There had been no mention of taking a boy when he had talked with Bob earlier.

Jim met Bob, and they discussed the problem. Jim was not real happy that Joey had been brought back to Brownwood. He was afraid of being found out, especially when it came to kidnaping.

That could lead to real trouble. Bob insisted that the boy was the only one in the pasture, and he just didn't know what to do since they knew he had seen them. Jim went over everything the boy had said. He didn't mention his dad. He was only worried about his mom and sister. Surely there weren't any missing pieces. Joey did say he had not seen their faces good enough to tell what they looked like. He didn't mention seeing the license number and the cows did not have any brands on them. That was understood before hand. Maybe he needed to talk to Wesley. If only Bob and Jake had left the kid.....this could be more trouble than he wanted.

Chapter 9

Sam went to his office early. He had not gotten much sleep. Sara had been so upset, and Betty, his wife, had insisted Sara stay at their house. Sara cried most of the night. The stolen cows were one thing, but Joey being gone was something else. Sam had a friend, L. D. Cooper, that was in the Texas Rangers, and he wondered if he needed to call them. He had never worked a kidnap case before and he was just sure that was what had happened. Joey must have seen the men loading the cows and somehow tried to stop them. Sam was pretty sure the boy was not in the pasture. The dog would have been close to where he was, if Joey was still in the pasture. Just to be sure, Sam and Dan would walk the pasture again this morning, just as soon as it was daylight.

L. D. Cooper wondered what Sam could want. Early on a Thursday, he told his boss he was going to be out of touch for a day or two. He wasn't sure how long he would be gone. It could be for pleasure or it could be business. He just needed to see what Sam wanted.

Coop, as everyone called him, parked next to Sam's car and went in. Sam had someone in his office, so Coop waited out in the hall. When the man left, Coop went back in and knocked on Sam's door. "Come on in," he called. Coop opened the door, and Sam said "Boy, am I glad to see you. Come on in and sit down." They had small talk, and talked of old times, then Sam said, "Coop, I needed you to listen and look over some things I've got here."

It took the rest of the day for Sam to go over everything that had happened, and to show the evidence he had been able to collect. Coop was careful to take all kind of notes, and ask questions. Then he said he wanted to talk to Bevi. "Oh, Coop," Sam said, "Bevi isn't even old enough to go to school. Sara has been through so much, I just hate to put anything else on her." "I know, Sam," said Coop, "but there are some gray areas here, and I need all the information I can get if we are to break this and find that boy." Sam knew he was right.

Sam's car turned into the gate just as Sara finished with the milking. Sam introduced Coop, and Sara invited them in. While Sara put the milk away, Bevi showed Sam and Coop the new kitten and told Sam about the red bird that had a nest in the tree in the back yard. Sara poured some lemonade for Bevi and coffee for the men. Then she looked at Sam and said, "I know this is not just a visit, Sam, is this good news or bad about Joey?" Sam smiled and tried to be cheerful. "Sara, Coop just wants to ask Bevi some questions. You know, he is a Ranger and I feel this whole thing is bigger than I first thought." Sara nodded and said, "I don't know what else she can add, but we will do anything to find Joey." Coop took out his pad and pencil, and sat down by Bevi. "Now Bevi, can you tell me about the pickup and just what you and Joey saw?" Bevi thought real hard and tried to tell everything. She told about the big pipe, the sand, the noise that scared her, and when she talked about hiding in the trees with Joey, she cried. It was so lonesome without Joey.

As they were leaving, Sam thanked Sara for everything, and told Bevi she did good. Bevi seemed awfully sad. She missed Joey so much. Sara rocked her to sleep that night.

Sara woke with a start. She had dozed off just sitting in the chair reading. Goodness, what time was it? Was that a noise she had heard? Oh, no, probably just the wind she thought. She was far too jumpy lately. She made sure all the doors were locked, then she checked the time - 3 A.M. - not a good time to be just going to bed, she thought. She missed having Rags there to bark, and it was so hard not knowing where Joey was.

Sara had written to Carl, but had been careful to not mention Joey being kidnaped. She did not think that would be good for him to read about so far from home. She was standing by the mailbox, waiting for the mail carrier to arrive. She really hoped there would be a letter today. “Good morning, Paul” she called, as the mail car pulled up. “I decided to just wait on you today.” “Good morning, to you Ms. Sara” said the mail carrier, “I sure wish I had that special letter for you - but there ain’t none today either.” She was sad, but tried hard to not let it show. “Oh well, Carl just probably has not had a chance or something. I’m sure everything is alright.” Sara said. “Have a good day, Paul.” “You too, Ms. Sara,” he said and drove off.

Chapter 10

Jim Fleming had a sleepless night. He had to get that boy away from Fran and Dave. If the boy remembered anything, he didn't need anyone else to hear it right now, least of all Fran Gray. He decided his best chance was to just go get him. Jim drove up to the Gray farm and stepped out of the car. Dave was coming in from the barn. "Hey Dave, how are you?" Jim called out. "Just fine, Jim. Come on in the house for some coffee. Fran was just waking up the boy." Jim, Dave and Fran sat down for coffee just as Joey came down the hall. "Good morning, Joey" Fran said. "Would you like some breakfast now?" Joey nodded his head and sat in the only other chair at the table. Fran got up and fixed Joey a plate of eggs and bacon and toast.

"Joey," said Jim, "I was wondering if you remembered anything else about those men?" "No, sir," said Joey, "I was so scared, I guess I just don't remember. I don't think I ever saw them before." "Now,

now, Joey," said Fran, "I can understand that. You have had a real scary experience." She turned and looked Jim in the eye and said, "This is just a child. I do not want him pushed on this. When he remembers, he will tell you." Dave started to say something, but decided Fran was not in any mood to listen. Jim looked at Dave and then back at Fran and said, "You are exactly right, Mrs. Gray. I'm sorry Joey. I didn't mean to push you. I was just anxious to get this settled so you could go home." Joey eyes brightened at that. "I would sure like to go home," he said. "Well, just maybe that can be arranged." said Jim. "This friend of mine is going to Abilene today, and if we could catch him, you could ride with him. That way, you would be home with your folks, and if I needed you, I could let the Sheriff there know." "I could go home today?" asked Joey. "That's what I mean." Jim looked at his watch and said, "We need to hurry though, to catch him. I think he plans on leaving in an hour or so."

Joey cleaned his plate in a hurry, went back to the bedroom where he had slept, and made up his bed. He knew mom would want him to do that. Joey was ready pretty quick. He thanked Dave and Fran for helping him, and as he started off the porch, he turned and hugged Fran. "Thank you," he said, and ran for the Sheriff's car.

Jim turned the car down the highway, and Joey settled back. Jim was a little worried about several things. What to do with the boy was just one of them. They had gone about ten miles when the car slowed down. Joey looked around, and said, "Is this the way?" Jim shook his head and said, "I need to check on something before I leave the county." As they neared the house, Joey saw some trailers, and some other pickups parked at the barn. When he had parked the car, Jim said, "Come on kid, I want you in the house." He opened the door without knocking and put his hand on Joey's shoulder.

The house didn't have much furniture. Just some chairs and a table with sacks and cans on it. Joey felt a little scared, but tried to not let it show. He just was not sure he liked this Sheriff, he sure acted different from Sheriff Sam. Joey was trying hard to understand what was happening. About that time, the door opened and a man came in. He wondered if this was the man going to Abilene. He had a beard, and his clothes and boots were dirty. Jim Fleming looked at him and said, "I want the kid to stay here. He needs to stay in the house until I get back. Is that understood?" "Sure Boss," said the other man. "I think we can handle that." Joey slowly turned to look at the voice he heard. He had heard that voice before. "Well I hope you can. Seems there is some questions about how things have been handled the past few days," Jim Fleming was saying. "Now, Boss, it all happened so fast, I just didn't know what else to do." "Well, we will just need to look real close at everything," said Jim. As he turned to leave, Jim looked at Joey and said, "Now you stay put, and do what Bob says. Do you understand?" "Ye-Yes sir," said Joey. Bob shoved him into a chair and said, "I'll be right back. You stay put."

Joey was scared, but he sat where he could see out the window as Bob and the Sheriff walked out to the car. He could tell both men were kinda mad. Joey knew this was the voice he had heard when he was put in the pickup. He had never seen his face before, but he remembered the voice. He was so scared his legs were shaking. He had to act like he didn't recognize the voice. He had to stop shaking. What would Dad do? He decided to just do what ever they said. Maybe somehow, he could get away again and find his way home.

After the Sheriff drove off, Bob came back into the house, and said, "come with me kid." They went out the back door and up to a storage building. There weren't any windows that Joey could see, and as Bob opened the door, he shoved Joey inside, and slammed the door shut. Joey heard it latch from the outside. "Hey, what are you doing?" Joey yelled. "It's alright, kid, I'll be back in an hour. You just stay where you are." Bob replied.

It was dark in the building except for some light coming in around the door. Joey had a long time to think about all that was happening. He thought about Bevie, and Mom and Dad, and wondered how he could get home. It was hard to keep from crying. He missed Rags and Mom and Bevie. Wiping the tears from his eyes, Joey knew he had to just do as he was told, and maybe there would be a chance for him to slip away again.

Jim Fleming drove back to the highway and turned north. After about two miles there was a dirt road to the right. He turned onto the road and drove several miles to the back side of the pasture where he parked and got out. He walked around the tank and up to a house from the back. This was the only way in except for the main highway and no one had used that road in years. Since there was so much traffic, Jim had fenced across the lane a couple of years ago. It was an old farm house. He went straight to the room with the two way radio. "Come in Bluebird. Come in. Over". He waited for a reply....when none came, he said again "Bluebird, Come in. Over." Then a voice came back. "This is Bluebird, Over." Jim picked up the microphone and flipped the switch. "We got a problem here, and I need your help. Over." The voice came back, "What kind of a problem do we have? Over." Jim wanted to be sure on all points and needed some advice. "The boys brought in some,... ah, ah, cargo two days ago. They were seen loading the last bunch. The cargo got away from them, but has been found. I took it to Bob. Over" There was a long silence, then Bluebird said, "I'll need to talk with you. Where are you? Over." "I'm at JBF right now. Over." "I'll be there in an hour. Over and out." said Bluebird.

Joey had made up his mind not to cry no matter what. He had to get away from here. What would Sheriff Sam want him to do? He had to be calm and remember everything. It was a long time before the man called Bob got back. He unlocked the door and took Joey by the arm. They went into the house and he told Joey to sit at the table. After a few minutes, Joey heard a car or pickup. Bob went to the door. He turned and looked at Joey. "Not a word out of you, do you understand?" "Yes sir" Joey said. By this time Jim Fleming was coming into the house. He looked around, and motioned for Bob to step outside. "Anything going on?" he asked. "Not a thing. He's been quiet as a mouse." Bob said. "What are we gonna do with him?" Jim was not real happy with the circumstances, but knew they had to work with it. "Well," Jim said, "we are going to take him over to the Lucky S and leave him with Old Man Sims for awhile. After dark, I want you to tie a sack over the kid's head, and carry him over there. By that time, Sims will know he's coming and he knows to keep his mouth shut." Bob grinned and said, "Old man Sims ain't smart enough to talk. You can tell him anything and he just nods and says, 'Yes sir.'" "Sims ain't the only one that's not very smart," snapped Jim. "I don't want any slips this time. Do you understand?" "Sure Boss, whatever you say, I'll do" replied Bob.

Jim Fleming went back into the house and told Joey he would be back at dark. "I'll bring you something to eat, okay?" Jim said. "Okay." said Joey. "Then are you going to take me home?" "Well, Joey, I have a little problem right now. We need to put that off a day or two. But you just do as you are told, and everything will be alright." Jim said. He nodded to Bob and left. Joey watched him drive off. He looked real hard. He wanted to remember everything about the pickup and the house.

Chapter 11

Coop and Sam talked long into the night. Coop just knew there was something there that he was missing. Sam was going over all his notes and he looked up and said, "Coop, do you reckon the Cattleman's Association might be of some help? You know we might look at the stolen cattle reports. It's slim but at least it might turn up something." Coop thought a minute and then said, "That's a good idea. Do you have a local here?" "Sure, just a small office but at least it's a start." Sam replied. The two of them decided to call it a night.

The next morning found Sam in the Cattleman's Association Office. He asked for copies of the stolen cattle reports. The girl was busy making copies when Coop came in. "Thought I'd find you here," he said to Sam. "Any luck yet?' "I haven't looked yet. I thought we'd take it back to the office," Sam said. "Good," said Coop. Both men looked over the reports and made notes, then compared what they had found. "You know, I see mostly young stuff being taken, and if you notice, it's in a pretty big circle. I can't put my finger on any one thing yet." Sam said. "You're right," said Coop. "It doesn't make a connection yet." "Have you put the boy's description out?" Coop asked. "No, I don't want to put Joey in danger, but neither do I want these guys to get by with this," Sam said. "Sam," Coop said, "I hate to ask this, but could that boy be in one of those tanks?"

"No," said Sam. "I didn't want to alarm Sara, but Dan and Ted dived both tanks. There was nothing. I just never mentioned it. Sara is holding up good, and I just didn't mention that to her. But we did look in all the tanks. Not even a foot print." "That's good," said Coop.

Chapter 12

Joey knew this was going to be a bad night. It looked like a storm was coming up and he could hear thunder in the distance and it kinda smelled like rain. Bob came in the room at dark and gave him a burger and some water. When he had finished eating, Bob tied his hands and put a sack over his head. Joey was so scared. “What are you doing that for?” he asked. “The Boss told me to.” Bob replied. “We’re going on a little short trip and this is how you are to go.” “Now start walking. There ain’t nothing in front of you. Here, step off the porch,” Bob said. He took Joey by the shoulder. He stumbled some, but Bob grabbed him. Then he said, “Here’s the pickup. I’m going to put you in the back.” “Where are you taking me?” asked Joey. “Just don’t you worry, it won’t take long.” said Bob. Joey heard the side-board gate close and the cab door open and close. He moved to the front and sat down. The pickup began to move. Through the sack, he could hear the thunder, and every now and then catch a flash of lightening. They went over some real bumpy roads. Joey heard tree limbs brush on the side of the pickup. There were so many turns, Joey could not keep up with them.

Finally the pickup stopped and Bob told Joey to get out. He nearly fell when he got down since his hands were tied and a sack was over his head. Bob caught him and held him tight against the pickup. He untied Joey's hands, and took the sack off. His eyes adjusted to the dark and he could make out a house over next to the trees. There was the smell of rain and the clouds were black and rolling. When the lightning flashed, Joey could see some of the buildings. There was an old man coming out the door of the house. He looked crippled or something.

"Come on," Bob said, "this is where you are going to be for a few days. I don't want you running off either, do you hear me, boy?" "I hear you," Joey replied. "How could I run off anyway. I don't know where I am?" "Now don't you get smart with me. I ain't gonna take that off a kid," snapped Bob. He pushed Joey ahead of him and pointed him toward the house. About that time, Joey saw a dog and heard him growl. "It's alright, dog." said the man. "Sims, this here is Joey. You are to keep him for a few days. The Boss said you are to not let him out of your sight. Do you understand?" asked Bob. "Yah, yah. I said I would," said Sims. Bob shoved Joey toward the man. "I'll be back kid, and you better be here." he said, as he turned and headed for the truck.

Boom! The thunder sounded so close it made Joey jump. "Come on in, young man," said Sims. "We'll get wet if we stay out here." They went into the house and dog followed. After Sims lit the lamp, he motioned Joey to a chair. "Don't be scared. I ain't gonna hurt you. I'm a prisoner myself." "Ah, a prisoner?" asked Joey. "I- ah,- I'm just scared and the Sheriff is gonna take me home in a few days." Sims laid his hand on Joey's shoulder and said, "I wouldn't believe that if I were you, son. Those men can not be trusted. But it's alright. No one will hurt you here. Dog there don't like'em and when I tell him, he's gonna rip their arms plum off." Joey heard the rain start to fall. "What's your name boy?" asked Sims. "Joey Thomas, sir." he said. "Sims is mine. You can just call me that. Sims. That will do fine. And that there is Dog." There was only one big room . On one side was a stove with a table in the middle. On the other side was a bed. Sims set up a cot for Joey, and told him they were safe. "No one will bother you as long as I'm around" he told Joey.

Chapter 13

Dave and Fran were having lemonade on the front porch. It was so cool and the night air had a smell of rain. It would sure be nice if it rained. They needed it so bad. Fran reached her hand to Dave and said, "Dave, I just can't get that little Joey off my mind." "I can't either," said Dave. "I went by Jim's office today while I was in town, but his door was locked. The girl across the hall said he hadn't been in all day." Fran was so tender hearted, and she loved children. Joey had been so young. "I would sure hate for that to be my little boy and not know where he was. His mother has got to be worried sick." Dave was quite for a long time. "I wonder who that friend of Jim's was that was going to Abilene?" He said. "I wanted to ask him" Fran said, "but decided it was best to not say anything." Dave knew how Fran felt about children. They had lost their boy when he was just a teenager. They were never able to have any other children. She really hurt for that boy. If there was anything he could do to ease her pain, he wanted to do it. Dave just did not know of anyway to check on Joey. After all, they had not gotten his parents name or anything. Things had just happened too fast. Maybe they could check the newspaper. Surely a kidnapped child would be reported.

Jim Fleming knew he needed to stop by Dave Gray's house and tell them Joey was alright. He didn't want Fran to start asking questions. Neither did he want them to remember something Joey had said and him not know it. He decided to drop by and talk with them.

"Why Jim," said Dave, "come on in." "Oh, I really don't have time. I just wanted you to know that Mike called and said Joey was sure glad to get home." "Oh, I'm so glad to hear that," said Fran. Jim started to leave, then stopped and said, "By the way, did you happen to get his folks name. I guess I didn't ask or at least I didn't write it down." "No, we didn't" said Dave. "His father is in the service and their last name is Thomas. That's all we know." Jim nodded his head, "Thomas is all I remember" he said. Fran watched as he drove down the lane. As she remembered it, Jim Fleming had not asked Joey about his parents or any real detail.

Sims woke early and put on the coffee. He puttered around the stove, and kept an eye on Joey. "That boy don't look very old," he thought. "He is tall alright, but his face and eyes look so young. Kinda heavy on the young too." He poured himself a cup of coffee, and stepped outside. Dog nudged his leg and he reached a hand and petted him on the head. Sims was deep in thought. Just how long had he been here? Well, now this was the second summer. They, especially that one called Bob, were a mean bunch. He knew they were stealing cattle. He just didn't know how to do anything about it. There was that one that wore the Sheriff's badge and carried the gun and the other one that wore the fancy clothes. He was not as mean acting as the others, and Sims felt he could be the boss but was not real sure. Now Sims had kept dates and descriptions of all the cattle that passed through the lots there. He had found some with holes punched in their ears, and there had been others with a notch, and some with no markings at all. All of this was kept on a pad, and the pad was under a loose board under his bed. Last night, after the boy had gone to sleep, he had pulled the pad out, and made note of the date and just what had happened.

The door opened, and Dog wagged his tail. "Morning," said Sims, as Joey stepped out. "You alright boy?" he asked. "Yes Sir, I am, but my name is Joey." Sims smiled, "Okay, Joey. Would you like some breakfast? You will have to drink coffee or water. I ain't got no milk," he said. Joey was glad to have anything. He was thirsty and hungry and whatever he was cooking, it sure smelled good. After they ate, Sims had to tend the stock. Joey went to the barn with him. Before they reached the barn, Sims said, "Joey, just do what I do, and help me carry the feed, put water where it belongs, and check to make sure all the gates are closed." "We will talk more when I'm sure it's just me and you. A person can never be to careful.

They may have one of them listening devices hid somewhere." Joey nodded and reached for Dog.

Chapter 14

Nearly a week since Joey arrived and it was just Sims and Joey and Dog. They were careful to not talk or show any indication of seeing what was going on. Sims had cautioned Joey, and showed him how to act. Joey had found a peep hole at the barn where he could see the road where the pickup came. He and Dog wondered around the barns and close around the house. They were becoming good friends.

Joey and Dog were in the barn looking for a bird's nest one evening when he heard the pickup. He moved over to the wall and sat down where he could see through his peep hole. He watched as the men loaded up the cows - even Old Bessie. They didn't leave any. Joey could see the pickup and he could also see the license plate. He took a stick and scratched the numbers on the wall. When all the cows had been loaded, they talked to Sims a few minutes; then Bob hit Sims in the face. Dog was with Joey or Bob wouldn't have done that.

Sims fell to his knees, and then he got up. He said something to Bob, but the Sheriff stepped between them. Joey was too far away to hear what they were saying. The Sheriff pointed his finger at Sims, and said something then he patted the gun and then his badge. He pointed to all the barns. Then he turned and got in the pickup.

Joey stayed where he was until he was sure they were gone. Then he scrambled out of the barn and hurried to Sims. "Are you hurt? Why did he hit you?" he asked. Sims had finished with the water. He put his arm around Joey, and said "I'm fine. I'm just glad you stayed out of sight." "But why did he hit you?" Joey asked again. "Well, I told them I was going to turn them in to the law." Sims said. "That's when Bob hit me and said now I had reason to. The Sheriff said I'd have to turn them in to him and that if I did, he would shoot me and tell everyone that I was the one stealing the cattle." Joey looked at Sims and said, "I copied the license number down." "You did?" said Sims. "I forgot to even look. Where is it?" "I'll need some paper. I put it on the wall in the barn," said Joey. "I'll get it for you," said Sims.

When they got to the house, Sims gave Joey some paper and pencil, and sent him back to the barn. While he was gone, Sims took his pad and wrote down all that had happened. When Joey got back, he added the license number. Dog barked. Joey went to the window. "They're coming back down the road." "Hide that piece of paper and stay out of sight," Sims said as he stepped out the door.

Joey watched as the Sheriff got out of the pickup. Sims walked toward him and said, "What do you want now?" "Well," the Sheriff said, "I just wanted you to know that I meant what I said." Sims was looking him in the eye. "I understand that, Sheriff, but you got to understand something too. You've had me held prisoner here now for right near three years and there are some things that a man really gets tired of. I intend to see you and that bunch of men burn. It was okay that you put me here. I didn't have nobody anyway, and was too drunk most of the time to care, but that boy is something else. He has a family that's looking for him and don't have no idea where to look. That's pure wrong. I don't rightly know how or what I'm gonna do, but it will happen."

The Sheriff stepped closer and said, "Has he told you where his folks are or anything about them?" "No, not a word, but he will one of these days, and I will try to help him." said Sims. Jim Fleming started to move closer to Sims and Dog growled and ran between them. "Stop, Dog," said Sims. "I could kill that dog right now," said Jim. "I wouldn't put my hand on that gun, if I wanted to keep it," said Sims. Dog was ready to attack. He didn't want anyone hurting his master. Jim backed off and said, "I'll be back when you least expect it. By the was, where is the boy?" "He's in the house," said Sims. The Sheriff turned and walked to his pickup. Sims and Dog stood and watched as he drove down the road.

Sims turned and went into the house. It was time to talk straight with the boy. He sat down at the table and said, "Joey, I ain't worth much, and I ain't never tried to help nobody. That dirty bunch talked me into coming out here and watching their cows. I was to ask no questions, and I had to stay here all the time. I didn't have no place to live and the Sheriff picked me up off the streets in Houston. I was just a plain drunk bum, that's all, a drunk bum. Now me and you gotta do something or they are going to kill us. They will do that too." Joey tried to keep from shaking. He was scared. "Kill us? You mean really kill us?" asked Joey. "I sure wish Sheriff Sam was here, he could do something; I just know he could." Joey said.

Sims was going through the cabinet, and then he reached under his bed and got a sack. "How about, if you and me and Dog pack our stuff, gather up the food and get out of here?" Joey tried to talk but his voice just wouldn't sound. "We will make a bedroll and sleep under the stars. When we find the highway, we'll flag a car and ask them to take us to your folks place." Sims was saying. Joey thought for a second and said, "You don't know the way out of here either?" "No," said Sims. "I had a sack over my head, just like you, when they brought me in here."

Sims fixed them a quick meal while Joey gathered up the supplies and put them in the sack. Then they made bedrolls out of the blankets. Sims turned the lights out and told Joey to be real quiet. They were going to just wait for awhile. He wanted to make sure they were not being watched.

Just after midnight, Sims told Joey it was time to head out. Sims had taken his pad out of the hole and it was in his sack. They went around the back of the house and into the woods. There was a lot of grass so there was no danger of leaving a lot of tracks. It was about an hour before they came upon a creek. It was pretty full of water. The moon was bright, and Sims said, "Let's wade in the water awhile. That way there won't be no tracks." The water felt good. They went down stream, or at least that is what Sims said they were doing. Sims found some rocks and they got out on the rocks and sat down and rested some. Dog laid his head on Joey's leg. "He likes you," said Sims. After a bit he said, "Well, now, come on, let's find us a hidie hole for the rest of the night."

They walked around very quietly, finally Sims found some logs that had fallen in a clump of trees. He and Dog walked around and decided it was a good place. They unrolled their bedrolls, and put the sack of food against the log. It wasn't long before Joey was asleep.

Sims woke up just as day was breaking. He sure wanted a cup of coffee, but knew he couldn't start a fire. Someone was bound to see it. He opened a small can of beans and woke Joey. "Ain't much, but I bet you never had beans for breakfast before," he chuckled. Joey rubbed his eyes and looked around. "No sir, I never did," he answered. After they had eaten, they rolled up the bedrolls and covered the bean can with dirt. Sims was careful to brush the grass where they had slept. He didn't need them to follow anytime soon. They were headed north when the sun came up. Sims didn't know where he was but he was sure there had to be a house or a road of some kind, if they kept going north.

Jim Fleming was up early and decided to go back and talk to Bob and Jake. He was afraid that boy might start remembering things. Something had to be done with the kid and old man Sims. When he got to the JBF farm house, he found Bob and Jake having coffee. They talked for awhile. Then Jim said, "We've got to get rid of Sims and the kid. Stealing is one thing but kidnaping is another. I don't want them to be found anywhere around this part of the country. Do you understand?" "Sure," said Bob, "but just how are we going to get them out of the county or state for that matter?" "I don't know. That's what we need to talk about," said Jim. They discussed several options and a lot of 'what ifs' but Jim objected to each one. Finally Bob said, "Just how many know about that place where Sims is?" "I don't know, my guess would be not very many. At least no one that I know. It has been vacant for years, as far as records in the county go," said Jim. He thought a few minutes. Then he said, "it would be a long time before anything was found back in that back section. There's a lot of trees and brush. No road on any side. That would be nearly perfect." "Okay. Let's go get it done. You do the kid but remember.... Sims is mine," said Bob. They got in the pickup and headed out. It was still early, so they expected to find Sims and Joey at the house.

They found the place vacant. "Where could they be?" asked Jake. "Look around for them," said Jim. "They can't have gone far." After a bit, Jim said, "The dog's gone too." "We need to look for tracks or something" said Jim. They searched the barns, whistled for the dog, called for Sims and Joey, but there was no answer. After looking through the house, they still didn't have any idea where they were. All the food was gone, but the bed clothes were still there. "We need to scatter and find them. There has to be some tracks. Look close, they can't be far. Sims will probably head north. He will try to protect that boy too. So let's be sure there are no clues left," said Jim.

Chapter 15

Sims and Joey had walked a long time. They came to a fence and Sims decided they needed to cross over into the other pasture and keep going north. They were careful to not leave any unnecessary tracks. Sims saw that Joey was lagging behind, so he decided to stop and rest a bit. After all, he was just a boy. They sat down in a clump of trees. "Where are we going?" asked Joey. "Well, I think our best chance will be to get in touch with your Sheriff. What did you say his name was?" asked Sims. "Sheriff Norris," answered Joey. "But how are we going to do that? We don't even know where we are." said Joey. "Now, don't you worry too much about that. When we find the highway, there has got to be some cars go by. I'll wave one down, and we will ask which way to go," Sims said. Joey was scared, but he sure wanted to be home.

"Sims, what will they do if they find us?" Joey asked. "Well, Joey, I just don't know for sure," said Sims, "but the Sheriff said he would use his gun on me if I ever crossed him, and now that you have seen their faces, he will do the same thing to you." "You mean he would kill us? Really kill us?" asked Joey. "That's what he said," answered Sims.

They were quiet for a long time. Finally Sims reached into his bedroll and pulled out his notepad. "Joey, I want you to know, I have written down everything they have done for the past year. It's all right here on this pad. If they get me, I want you and Dog to take this pad, and stay out of sight, and get it to your Sheriff Norris. He's the only one I would trust right now. Do you understand what I'm saying?" asked Sims. "Ye-Yes sir, I think I do," said Joey, "but how will I find my way?" "Quiet, listen. What's that?" asked Sims. "Did you hear that? sounds like.." About that time Dog growled. "Quick! Into the brush, and lay low on the ground, don't move, and stay put.... no matter what...Dog!, you stay here," said Sims in a whisper. Joey crawled into the brush pile, and Dog followed him. He reached for his bed roll and pulled it in, just as he saw Sims run behind another clump of trees. Dog perked up his ears, but he didn't move. Sims had told him to stay. It sure sounded like the pickup motor. About that time, Joey noticed the pad Sims had been holding. It was laying on the ground. Joey knew he had to get that pad. He moved a little and looked all around. Dog was still but looking in the direction Sims had gone. Joey took a stick and reached as far as he could, he still couldn't reach the note pad. So he moved a little more. There, he had it. He pulled the pad under the brush and scooted it under his belly for right now.

He was so scared, his teeth were chattering. He had to stop it. Be still. He reached out and put his arm around Dog. He scooted a little closer to Dog. His ears were perked up and he was whining and growling at the same time. BOOM! BOOM! Dog jumped. He wanted to run to Sims, but he couldn't . He had to stay. Sims had said to stay.

Joey held tight to Dog. BOOM! Joey knew it was a gun. He lay still. Dog whined, then perked up his ears. Joey listened real hard. He thought he could hear that motor again. He did. It was coming closer. He moved backwards into the brush pile some more. "Come on Dog," he whispered. The pickup came into sight. It was moving real slow. Joey held tight to Dog, his heart was pounding. The man in the pickup drove closer, then he turned left and circled the brush pile. "What if he stops?" thought Joey. " What will I do?" They did not move. Dog laid real still, but he was watching the pickup. It kept moving from one clump of trees to another, but it always circled back to where they were. He seemed to know they were there. Joey was sure they were just teasing him...wanting him to run to Sims. But he wouldn't do that. He had to wait until he was sure they were gone, then do just what Sims had said.

Chapter 16

Bob was sure the boy and dog were in the area. The only problem, the dog was not with Sims. That could mean that Sims had left the boy and dog and slipped out by himself. Or he could have hidden them somewhere while he went to find help. Whatever, he was sure the dog was with the boy. He stopped the pickup and listened, then he whistled for the dog. He drove back to Sims' body and loaded it into the pickup. He would come back with food for the dog, that would bring them out. He was sure they were not far from where he found Sims. In fact, he would nearly bet Sims was heading toward them. That would have been down in that valley to the southwest. There was a small cave there, he had seen it before while chasing some calves. He would look there after he got Sims out of sight.

Joey lay still for a long time. He didn't hear anything, but he knew they needed to move on north like Sims had said. He took the pad and put it in his bedroll, and picked up the sack of food. "Come on, Dog," he said, "we've got to go." Dog didn't want to, but he followed. Joey ran from one clump of trees to the other. He had to stay out of sight. The sun was moving to his left, so he knew he had to keep going. He wanted to find a house before night. "Did you hear something?" he asked Dog. Dog's ears had perked up and he was standing very still. Joey hunkered down beside him and listened. It's a pickup - in front of them and to the left some - no it was now to the right - a road!, that's what it was - they had found a road. Joey picked up the sack and bedroll and ran to the next clump of trees. There were some big rocks and some brush. He moved around the rocks real slow. Another motor. It had to be a busy road. They finally moved around the rocks enough to see a highway. There was a fence then the highway. "What do we do now?" he said. Dog licked his hand and wagged his tail.

Joey found a place between the rocks where no one could see him from behind, and they would have to stop to see him from in front. He put his bedroll down and sat on it, then he took the food sack. Sims had put his big knife in the sack so he could open the cans. He tried and tried before he got the knife to cut the can. He was hungry and thirsty. There wasn't any water. He ate most of the beans. Then he poured the rest out on the rock for Dog. He licked it clean. He heard another car coming. He would sit real still and see who it was. There it was a shiny white car. He watched it for a long time, then it turned off the highway. Joey wondered how far from town they were. Goodness, he didn't even know the name of the town. The sun felt good, and he could smell wild flowers all around, and the gentle breeze felt so good. It had been a long time since he had slept in his bed. He leaned his head back against the rock. Dog laid his head on Joey's leg. His thoughts turned to home. "I sure wish Sheriff Sam was here" he said to Dog.

Chapter 17

Joey's head snapped up. "What was that?" BOOM! There it was again. He had been asleep. - BOOM! It was a gun! Where's Dog? "Dog," he yelled, "Dog!" That was a gun he was sure. Dog must have slipped off while he was asleep. "Oh, no! Not Dog too," he said to himself. Tears began to well up in his eyes. What was he going to do now. He had to think. What would Sims do?

Joey sat real still. He had to think. The shot had sounded behind him. He had to cross the road to the other pasture. Slowly he stood up and peeked around the rocks. He didn't see or hear anything. He picked up his bedroll and the food sack and crawled down the rocks to the fence. Once under the fence, he ran across the highway and quickly crawled under the fence on the other side and was out of sight. He scrambled up the rocks and found a place where he could see where he had been. He lay very still. "Oh, there's Dog," he said out loud. He started to whistle, but stopped. What if someone was following Dog? They would hear him. He scooted back under the tree limb just a little farther. He had to stay out of sight. That's what Sims had said. "Don't let anyone see you, and don't give my pad to anyone but your Sheriff Norris." Joey was sure going to try and do just what Sims said. There was movement over there! What was it? Oh, no, there was a man and there was Dog. The man was taking aim on Dog. BOOM!, BOOM! He was trying to kill Dog. Joey jumped up and whistled for Dog just as a car passed. The man had ducked behind the rocks. Joey got down and gathered up his stuff and started to run farther into the pasture. Joey looked back and there was Dog. They ran for a long time. He was getting tired, and his side was hurting. He stopped and crawled up under some trees. He needed to rest just a few minutes.

Dog lay down beside him. After a short rest, he started walking again. He knew he needed to find some place to spend the night. He sure did want a drink of water. Joey knew he needed to watch Dog's ears. They were not perked up, so he knew no one was close by. He was walking into the sun now. He didn't know why - that was just the way he started. He gradually moved back closer to the road. They walked for a long while and the sun was nearly down. Off to his right was a white house. He could see it through the trees. He started down the lane and decided to sit and watch for awhile. He didn't want it to be a house where one of those men lived. He found a nice cool shady spot and sat down. As he sat watching the house, Joey thought about Mr. and Mrs. Gray. He had asked for help, but things really turned out bad. He didn't think the Grays knew the Sheriff very well. He was not sure he wanted to ask for help again, but he still didn't know where he was.

Chapter 18

Mary Gates was busy cooking supper. Why had she cooked so much? The only thing to do would be to take a large plate to Mr. Brooks. He was alone now that his wife had passed on and might appreciate some food. Mary was a school teacher. She had lived in this house all her life. She was what you would call "an old maid school teacher." As long as her parents were alive, she had cared for them and taught school. It was good to have summer vacation, but she was always glad to be back in the fall. The children were so anxious to learn. She finished cleaning up the pots and pans, fixed a large plate of food for Mr. Brooks, picked up her purse and headed for the car. This wouldn't take long and Mr. Brooks was not getting around too well anyway. She needed to check on him more often.

Joey saw the car start down the lane. He moved behind a tree and watched. It looked like the white car he had seen earlier. A woman was driving alone. This would be a good time to get a drink of water. He could see the windmill and knew there had to be water. As soon as the car was out of sight, he left his bedroll and headed for the windmill. He and Dog drank a long time. It was so cool and tasted so good. OOPS! Did he hear a car? There it was, he ducked down but was sure he had been seen. The woman got out, and went into the house. Maybe his luck was changing. He needed to figure out a way to get back to his bedroll without being seen.

Mary went into the house and turned her radio on. Mr. Brooks had asked about a child that had run away from home. He kept his radio on most of the time. He said they had broke into a program and said the boy was missing and if you saw him, to call the Sheriff. Now Mary wondered about that. Whose child was it? They did not give a name. Had it been one of her own? They gave the local news and then there it was. "A boy, age nine, had been reported missing. If anyone sees him, please call Sheriff Fleming. It was possible that he had a large dog with him." Poor child, he didn't need to be out alone. How long had he been missing? She would keep the radio on and hope to hear more. She wondered who he was.

Joey stayed behind the windmill tank. It was going to be dark pretty soon. "What's that? Oh no, another car," he said to himself. What was he going to do? When the car stopped, Dog started that low growl in his throat. Joey put his arm around his neck and whispered, "Ssh. We don't want them to hear us. Ssh, be quiet." He heard someone say, "Hello, ma'am, how are you?" Joey remembered that voice. It was the Sheriff Jim Fleming. Joey sat still and held on to Dog. He sure didn't want any noise to be made. "We are looking from farm to farm for a missing child," he said. "Have you seen anyone? There is probably a dog with him." "No, I haven't seen anyone, and I've been here most of the afternoon," the woman said. "Whose child is it? Do you have a name?" "To be real honest with you," he said, "I don't know whose child it is. His name is Joey." "I got the message over my radio, but I was nearly out of range. It was not a clear message. Since I was in this part of the county, I started going to all the farms along the highway." Mary shook her head, "Poor child, it's getting dark. I hope someone finds him soon," she said.

"Do you have any buildings around he could get in?" asked the Sheriff. "No, just the chicken house over there, and I was in there about an hour ago and closed and latched the door."she said. "There aren't any other buildings around anymore." The Sheriff thanked her, and asked her to call if she happened to hear anything, and got in his car and left. Mary stood watching as he drove off. There were a lot of questions that he had not answered. Who took the missing child report? Did they not get a name? She shook her head and reached for the door. My, my, the mother must be worried. Just nine years old. He would be in my class next year.

Joey and Dog sat still. They did not dare move. Joey was scared of being seen, and then he would be turned over to Sheriff Fleming again. He did not want that. As soon as it got dark, he ran from the windmill tank behind the chicken house. Dog came too. Now all he had to do was get back to his bedroll and the sack of food.

He crawled through the fence and into the pasture and started toward the tree where he had left his things. He had the pad that Sims had written on with him. He had been looking at it when the woman left. It was hard to read Sims writing. Dog growled and stopped. Joey got down beside him and looked in the direction Dog was looking. He couldn't see anything but Dog just kept that low growl in his throat and didn't move. Joey moved behind a tree and peeked around. They were nearly to the place where his bedroll was. Joey kept looking and looking, but there was nothing. Then he saw the headlight. It was coming down the lane to the house. It was the pickup that Bob drove. Joey made a mad dash for his bedroll. Dog watched the pickup as it went by real slow.

Joey picked up his bedroll and sack, and hurried back to Dog. As he neared the clump of trees he heard voices. Joey lay on his belly and looked around. The woman was talking to Bob. They were coming out of the chicken house. "You see," she said, "there is no one here." "I would have known if a child was around." she said. Bob looked around and flashed his light everywhere. "We sure need to find him." he said. "I'm just sure the people who saw the boy and dog said they came down your lane. They gave a real good description." Mary was a little out of sorts with the man. "You are certainly free to look anywhere. But if that child had come to me, I would have had to help get him home. It is dangerous for a child to be alone out there at night. How old did you say he was, nine years old?" "Yah, yah, that's what they said, nine years old," said Bob.

He started back to the pickup, and he shined his light right at the clump of trees where Joey lay. He moved on around the pickup and said, "I got a funny feeling you ain't telling all you know woman." He looked at Mary and she said, "I've told you all there is to tell." He grunted and opened the pickup door. "If he shows up, you'll call the Sheriff, if you know what's good for you," he said. Then he drove off. Mary watched him all the way down the lane.

Chapter 19

That settled that. Joey could not ask her for help. He could nearly taste that food he had smelled. He was pretty sure it was Bob that shot Sims, and Joey was sure he would shoot anyone that crossed him. As soon as the woman went into the house, Joey circled way around the chicken house and headed on west. There would be a place to stop somewhere. He would have to do like Sims and find a good hidie hole.

Mary was startled at the crude way the deputy had acted. She had never had anyone talk so impolite. It really seemed to her that he was threatening her too. Just what did he mean when he said "If you know what's good for you?" She locked the door. Something she had never done. It would be bad if that man found the child. Oh, how his mother must be hurting right now.

Joey came up on a clump of rocks that had some small trees and brush scattered around it. He and Dog walked and looked and finally found a way to the inside of the trees. Joey put down his bed roll and rolled it out. He was too tired to be hungry. He would eat later. He stretched out and Dog lay down by him and put his head on Joey's arm. Joey petted his head and said, "Now don't you go wondering off. We've got to find our way home." Dog whined and licked Joey's hand. It wasn't long before Joey was sleeping.

The next morning found Mary still wondering about the missing child. She went to let the chickens out and put out some water. "What is that - a foot print in the mud?" It was a small foot print. She followed them back to the windmill tank. There, it looked like someone had gotten a drink of water. Mary looked around, thinking maybe she would see him. "It sure wouldn't do for that deputy to see this," she said. She grabbed a rake and started raking the leaves and trash. She worked over an hour, all the while looking around to see if there were any other signs. If only that child had knocked on her door.

Mary was about to go into the house when she saw a car coming. It was the Sheriff. She got the wheelbarrow and started loading the trash. Sheriff Fleming came around the fence and said, "Good morning, Ma'am. You are at work early today." "I like to get this kind of work done before it gets very warm," she replied. "My deputy told me he was here last night." Jim said. "Yes, he came after dark. He wouldn't take my word for it. He had to look in the chicken house himself. He is a very rude man," Mary said. "I would like for you to know, I have never been talked to like that before." "I'm real sorry ma'am, my men have been a long time without relief, and I guess he was just trying to be sure that boy was found," he said. She finished loading the wheelbarrow and started for the house. "Would you like some coffee?" she asked. Thinking that might soothe her feelings, and he did want to look around the house, he said, "That would sure taste good, ma'am."

Jim Fleming left Mary's house convinced she knew nothing about the boy. He had looked all around and had even gone to the chicken house with her. There was nothing to suggest she was not telling the truth. Bob had been wrong as usual.

Now Jim had a strange feeling about several things. He knew Bob had killed Sims. The dog was still missing. Of course, the dog was not the problem. It was the boy. Could that boy find his way home? Who would believe his story anyway? He had told Dave and Fran Gray he had been kidnaped and the cows stolen. Was there any way the Grays could find the kid's folks? No, he didn't think so. He had checked all the newspapers, and there was no report of a missing child. The Grays would have to come to him to find out the Sheriff's name. He had been careful to check all the reports from the Breckenridge area. No one had reported a missing child. He wondered why, but maybe the kid did run away from home. All the cattle had been moved out to other places or sold. There was only the boy and the dog left, and they would be found he was sure. Maybe this was going to work after all. He just had to be careful and cover all areas.

Joey had slept hard. Dog was still by his side. Joey petted him and said, "We need to go." "I would sure like to find home today," he thought to himself. He looked in the sack. There were two cans of beans. He took the knife and finally punched a hole in the top. After they ate, Joey dug a hole and covered the can just like Sims had done. Then he wiped the knife clean and rolled it up in the sack and tied it in his bedroll. He took the pad out and looked at it. He decided to open his bedroll and put it there. No, that would not do. That would be the first place anyone would look if they found him. He thought and thought, then he took a piece of his blanket and made a collar for Dog. Then he tore the pages out and rolled them up in the cloth, then took a piece of the string from the sack and wrapped it around the collar real good. He tied it around Dog and said, "Now don't you lose that. It's all I got left of Sims." Dog seemed to understand what he had said. He whined and licked Joey's hand. When he was sure the collar would stay in place, they started out again Joey really wanted to get home.

Joey moved toward the sound of the highway. It was still early, the sun was coming up, and he wanted to cover as much ground as he could. Just one thing, he needed to find out which way to go. He kept hearing something like a big truck. He moved closer to the road to see what it was. Oh, gosh, they are working on the road. He watched a little while then he saw an older man looking at something. It looked like the map Sheriff Norris had. If that was what it was, it would tell him which way to get home. Now how did he get there and get to look at it? He thought and thought and then, he decided to play like he lived around here somewhere and go talk to the men. There was a mailbox. He would put a piece of paper in the mailbox. He dug in his pocket and found the pad. He tore out a piece of paper. He put the bedroll under a tree and tied Dog to the tree. "Stay!" he said to Dog. Dog whined, but he sat down on the bedroll.

Joey crawled through the fence started down the lane toward the pickup. He was whistling and reached down and threw a rock. When he got to the pickup, he said, "Morning sir. What you doing?" The man smiled and said, "Morning to you, young man. What are you doing out so early?" "Oh, my Mom just wanted me to put this note in the mailbox. She needs some stamps." By this time, Joey was standing on the fender looking inside the pickup. "Is that a map that tells you all the roads around here?" he asked. "Yes, it is" said the man. "Where are we? Can you show me where we are? I ain't never seen one of those," Joey said. The man was sipping his coffee, and he reached for the map and got out and laid it on the ground. "We are right here. See? You can go back down this way and get to Brownwood," the man said. Joey looked real hard, then he looked at the highway. "How do you know this mark on the map is the highway?" he asked. "Well, there is a number for every highway. You see this number right here in the circle? Well, it goes all the way through Texas." Joey looked real close. "Is that One eighty-three?" he asked. "That's right," said the man. He placed his finger on the map and traced the highway and said, "You see, you can follow this highway and there will be a sign by the road that has TEXAS 183 on it. That's this mark right here." "Gee," said Joey, "I never knew that. I gotta go tell Mom, I bet she don't know that either."

About that time, one of the men in the big trucks called him and the nice man had to leave. Joey stood and watched until they were out of sight. He hurried under the fence and back to Dog. He was sure proud he had found out how to get home. The man had followed the line with his finger and Joey had seen Gunsight by the line.

Chapter 20

Bob and Jake had orders from Jim to continue looking for Joey. They decided to split up and cover both north and south highways. Jim had said the boy would probably walk just inside the fence. They were to drive slow and keep a watch for the dog. That was when they would find the boy. They drove around most of the day and asked everyone they saw. No one had seen the boy or the dog. Bob was at the last road before the County line. He drove down it and looked around. There was a woman in the yard; she said she hadn't seen any stray dog or child. He turned around and headed back to the highway. He wondered if those men working on the road had seen anyone.

He had to back track about three miles. He stopped and asked if anyone had seen a kid and a dog. The foreman said the only kid he had seen was the one that went to the mailbox about three roads back. "Did he have a dog with him?" asked Bob. The man thought a minute and said, "No, he didn't have a dog. He came down the lane and put a note in the mailbox for his mom and we talked a bit." Bob seemed really mad. After he drove off, the foreman of the road crew remembered that the kid had not gone on to the mailbox. But then, he didn't have a dog either. Probably not the one they are looking for.

Joey and Dog stayed as close to the road as they could without being seen. Joey saw a sign by the highway, but he could not read it from where he was. He looked both directions and crawled under the fence and ran to see what it said. There it was TEXAS 183, just like the man said. He was so happy. They went back under the fence, and he picked up his bedroll and they were off.

Dog had his collar on and they were doing good. When they got tired, Joey found a small tank and got them a drink of water, then sat under a tree to rest. The day was passing fast. Joey was hungry, but didn't have anything but that one can. Maybe he needed to save it. He came to another fence, and saw it was a field of some kind. If he walked in the field, a car could go by and see him. There were some tall stalks off to his right in the field, it looked like corn stalks. He walked the fence until he got there and then he and Dog crossed under and walked down a row of corn to the other side of the field. After he had crossed into the next pasture, it dawned on him that there were some watermelons in the field. One would sure taste good. He put his bedroll down and crawled back under the fence.

He found one that looked pretty good. He pulled it and carried it to the fence, rolled it under, and then he crawled under. It was hard to carry the melon and his bedroll too.

After finding a shade tree, Joey took the knife and cut the melon. It was so good. He ate and ate. It had been several days since his stomach had been that full. Now, what to do with the rinds. He decided the birds and animals would eat them. So he picked up his bedroll and off they went again. This time there was a bounce to his walk. He was full and he was headed home.

Joey had checked all the way and he was still on Texas 183. There was a town up ahead. He wondered if he could just walk through and no one notice him. He had washed his face and tried to comb his hair at the last tank. He tucked his shirt tail in and put the rope from his bedroll on Dog. Then, he took the sack and put his blanket in it and carried it like he did when he helped Mom carry things at home.

There were a lot of people and he just walked right down the sidewalk. They were nearly out of town when he saw the pickup that Sheriff Fleming drove. He ducked into a store entrance real quick and just stood there looking. Dog growled real low. "I see him," Joey said. The owner of the store came up and said, "Just what are you shopping for, young man?" "Oh, nothing sir. I was just looking at this pretty lamp. My mom really likes pretty lamps." Joey said.

"Well, be on your way then and don't touch it, and take the dog out. I don't allow dogs in the store."

Joey pulled on the rope on Dog and they left the store. He stayed close to the buildings. At the edge of town, he looked at the signs again. After he was sure he was going the right direction, he started down the road. He heard a car coming, and so he ran for the fence. He couldn't get under. He was caught on the wire.

He pulled hard and finally got through, but the car had stopped and a man came to the fence and said, "Young man, come here to me. What are you doing on my land?" Joey was caught. He took a deep breath and went to the fence. "I'm just walking here sir," he said. "Who are you?" the man asked. "My name is Joseph Thomas, sir." The man held out his hand and said, "Claude Miles is my name." They shook hands and Mr. Miles said, "Where do you live?" "I'd, ah well, sir, up this way a little piece." "Well, hop in and I'll take you and your dog home," said Mr. Miles. "Oh, that's alright, me and Dog would rather walk than ride," said Joey. Claude Miles found that a little strange. Joey was not ready for the next question. "Why don't you and your dog come with me anyway? We will go to my house and talk about this. After all you are on my property." Joey took a deep breath, he knew he was caught and didn't think it was very good. But he didn't feel he had any choice except to get in the pickup. "Okay," said Joey, "come on Dog," he said. They got in the pickup and rode with Mr. Miles.

Claude Miles thought he could tell the boy was in trouble. He also knew he had never seen him around the town before. When they got to the house, Claude said, "Come on in son, I think Annie will have some milk and cookies for you." Joey wasn't very hungry, but some milk would sure taste good. Claude asked Annie to set out some milk and cookies.

"Now son," Claude said gently, "why don't we start again? Tell me again what your name is and just where you live." Joey sat on the porch looking down and trying to think of something to say.

Annie brought the milk and cookies and sat them on a small table. "Do we have a problem, Claude?" she asked. "I don't know," he replied. "I found this young man and his dog on our property. I don't think they live around here or at least I have never seen them." Annie reached over and touched Joey's head, and said, "If you have a problem, we could help you. Why don't you start by telling us your name?" Joey looked at her and said, "Well, I - ah- my name is ah, Joseph Thomas, but everyone calls me Joey, and this here is Dog." Claude picked up a cookie and said "You said you lived down the road a short way. Just how far down do you live? I can only think of one family around here by the name of Thomas. They don't have any children your age."

Claude was trying to be kind and gentle with his talk. He could tell Joey was scared, and looked like he hadn't had a bath in a long time.

"I sure wish you would tell me how to get in touch with your folks, or something. They must be pretty worried about you." he said.

Annie sat down in her chair. She reminded Joey of his Grandmother before she died. She had white hair, and her smile was soft, and she sure could make good cookies. Claude reached for another cookie and gave it to Dog. Then he said, "I heard on the radio yesterday that a boy about nine years old was missing. I wonder, was they talking about you?" Joey looked at him and then he ducked his head and said, "I don't guess I know what you're talking about."

Annie had been listening and watching and she said. "Claude, why don't you and Joey take some soap and towels and go to the barn tank. You two can swim and wash up. I'll have some of Grady's clothes ready when you get back. Joey is about the same size as our grandson." Claude said, "That sounds like a good idea to me. You want to go for a swim Joey?" "I don't swim too good" said Joey. "Dad was teaching me when he went to war. Mom don't like for me to swim without Dad." "Well, now, I can understand that" said Annie, "but Claude is a good swimmer, you will be just fine with him." "Is your father in service?" asked Claude. "Yes sir, he is in the army" Joey replied. They got up and Joey took the rope and Annie got the towels and soap.

Chapter 21

Joey seemed to relax some while they were swimming. Claude did not push him for information though. He needed to feel good and relax some. After their swim, Annie had laid out some clean clothes. They fit pretty good. There was a comb, and she even put out a toothbrush for him. Claude told him to gather up his dirty clothes. Annie would wash them.

Claude left the house and headed for the barn. Joey was still in the bathroom. When he came out, he looked around the living room. There on the wall were pictures of lots of people. He asked Annie where to put his dirty clothes. She showed him the laundry room. She was sure they needed to buy him some more. It looked like these had seen better days.

After their evening meal, Claude and Annie usually sat on the porch. Claude asked Joey if he wanted to feed the scraps to his dog.

"That would be good," he said. Claude was sure he started to say something else, but changed his mind. Annie raked all the scraps into one pan and said she would give him an old plate to eat out of. After the dishes were done, they all moved to the porch. Dog came around and laid down at Joey's feet.

Finally, Joey said, "Uh, Mr. Miles, uh sir, do you know the Sheriff named Jim Fleming?" Claude wondered what made him ask that, but he had to answer him. "Well, Joey, I've heard of him. I think he has his office in Brownwood. Why do you ask?" "Oh, I just wondered if you knew him?" Joey said. "Is he a friend of yours?" asked Annie. "Oh, no. He sure ain't no friend of mine," said Joey.

He answered so quick, Claude wanted to know more. "Is that why you don't want to tell us where you live, because of Sheriff Fleming?" Joey was sure he had talked too much. But now he had to know what they would do. "You gonna call the Sheriff if I don't tell you?" he asked. "No, Joey, I'm not going to call Sheriff Fleming. You don't have to worry about that," Claude said. Joey sat there and thought a long time. He could see the moon and the stars were out. It was sure a pretty night. It would sure be nice to be home. It had been a long time since he had seen Mom. The tears began to well up in his eyes.

Joey stood up and walked around the porch and out into the yard. He decided he really did need help to get home. So with his hands in his pockets, and his chin quivering he walked up to Claude and said, "Mr. Miles, you said you would help me if you could." "That's right Joey," said Claude. "I know you don't belong around here, and I know you are scared to trust anyone. I don't know why, but I can tell. Annie and I will help you get home, solve your problems, or do whatever we can, if you can just see your way clear to trust us." "Well, sir," said Joey, "I live, ah.... I live at Gunsight, and Sheriff Norris is our Sheriff. Do you know him?"

The tears in his eyes were about to fall, and he was having a hard time. Claude said, "Well, I just might. Are you talking about Sam Norris?" Joey nodded his head. "You are the boy they reported missing yesterday, aren't you?" "I don't know nothing about that. Me and Dog don't have no radio." Joey said.

Claude waited a few minutes and then he said, "If I can get Sam on the phone, would that make you feel better, Joey? You can talk to him yourself." Joey's eyes brightened up. He had never talked on the phone before, but he guessed he could do that. "Yes, sir, that would be good."

Claude got up, and they all went into the house. He went to his desk and got out a big book. After he had looked in the book, he said, "Here it is, Sam Norris, Sheriff." Claude took the phone and told the operator the number he wanted. In just a minute or two he said, "Hello, is this Sam Norris?" There was a pause and then he said, "I'm Claude Miles. Sam, do you remember me? Well, I'm just doing fine, but I have someone here that wants to talk to you."

He motioned for Joey and he told Joey to hold the phone to his ear and talk into this end. Joey was kinda shaking, but he took the phone, "Uh, Sher - Uh - Sheriff Norris, is that really you?" he said. Sam nearly dropped the phone. "Joey!, Joey! is it you? Joey, talk to me, please. Yes, I am Sheriff Norris," he said. "Where are you son? Are you all right? We have all been so worried about you." Joey's hand started shaking, and tears started to roll down his cheeks. It was so good to hear Sheriff Sam.

There was a lump in his throat and he was having a hard time with his voice. "I'm fine but - but I don't know where I am, except the road number is 183 and me and Dog have...ah..ah...been.... hiding and they shot Sims and...and I'm ....ah," Claude decided to help him out some. He reached and took the phone. "Sam, he is alright. You do remember me don't you?" "I sure do," said Sam, "but where is he? He has been missing now for over three weeks."

Claude explained just where he was, and assured Sam that Joey would be just fine until he could get there. Sam asked to speak with Joey again. "Joey, you can trust Claude. Do you understand me?" he asked. "Yes sir, I, ah.....I think so but ah...- but I got something that Sims told me to give to no one but you, and they shot him and tried to shoot me and Dog. We been hiding and running, cause I didn't know the way home and the Sheriff said he would take me and then he didn't and"... "Hey, hey," said Sam, "it will be alright. You have done good. You can give whatever you have to Claude, or you can hold it till I get there. Claude is a retired Texas Ranger. Do you know what that is?" Sam asked. "I'm not sure," said Joey as he sniffed and wiped his eyes. "Well, that is like a Sheriff, only he is called a Ranger. We are friends, you can trust him." said Sam.

After Claude hung the phone up, he put his arm around Joey and said "You sure had it rough for a boy. Do you want to talk now or do you want to wait for Sam?" Joey dried his eyes and said, "I got to get my stuff." He went out the door and picked up his sack, then he took the rope off Dog and untied the collar he had made. He hugged Dog and said, "It's okay now, Sheriff Sam will be here before long."

Sam had been about to leave the office. He was glad he had stayed a little late. He grabbed his hat, turned the lights out and locked the door. This was some news that Sara needed. He got in his car and headed for Sara's. She and Bevi were setting on the porch when Sam pulled up. Bevi ran to him and he picked her up and held her tight. As he stepped upon the porch, he held out his hand to Sara. "I talked to Joey about half an hour ago." Sara stood shaking, and crying and through her tears she said, "Is he hurt? Where is he? Will he be home tonight?" Sam worked hard to keep his own tears from falling. He explained where Joey was and that he was with a Ranger friend of his. He assured Sara that Joey was not hurt. From what he could tell, Joey had been through a pretty rough time, but had handled it well. "He will stay with Claude until I get there," Sam said.

Claude and Annie waited for Joey to untie his sack. He pulled the blanket out, and then the knife and can. There was a part of a note pad. There were some pieces of paper and Joey very carefully picked each one up and stacked them.

With tears rolling down his cheeks, Joey told Claude about the Sheriff saying he would take him home. And about Sims and how he had given him the note pad. He told how he thought Sims had been shot and how he had been at the lady's place and about Bob and how scared he was.

Joey was scared and yet so glad to be able to tell someone everything. He just cried and talked a long, long time. He couldn't make the tears stop falling. Annie went to him and cradled him in her arms. "Everything is going to be fine Joey. We are going to take care of you," she said. "You just cry all you want and when you are ready, I have a bed for you."

After a bit, Claude said, "Joey, you don't worry, tomorrow, when Sam gets here, we will talk about those men. They will be caught. No one is going to hurt you or Dog. You don't have to be scared any more." "Can Dog sleep in the room with me?" he asked. "He sure can," said Claude. Joey went to the door and let Dog in. When he was ready for bed, Dog lay down on the floor right by him.

Chapter 22

Claude and Annie took turns checking on them all night. He was so young and so scared. Sam arrived early the next morning with Coop. When Joey saw Sam, he ran to him and started crying and shaking all over. Sam held him close and assured him everything would be alright. "Can you take me home?" Joey asked. Sam smiled and said, "You bet, just as soon as we can get some facts down on paper."

Annie had some coffee and milk on the table. They all sat down and Joey said, "Mr. Sam, have you seen my Mom and Bevi?" "Yes I have," said Sam. "Your Mom wanted to come with us, but Bevi was a little under the weather. I really think she is missing her brother. Anyway we decided that I would bring you back with me." Joey smiled. "It will sure be awhile before I fuss at her for following me around," he thought to himself. It would be nice to hear her jabber. Now he could tell his story again. This time he started on the very first day, and told Sam everything he could remember. He named all the men, including the one that Sims had called Wesley, but Joey had only seen him one time.

Claude, Sam, and Coop talked a long time about the men. Claude felt sure they could get them arrested. All they had to do was find them. Joey was the only one that had seen them and he was just ten years old. Sam wondered just how much a Judge would believe. Claude suggested they drive around some and see if Joey could remember the road where he had been. Anything would help at this point.

Everyone got in Claude's car and they drove a long time. Finally, Joey said, "There it is, There's where I crossed the road and ran to those trees over there on that rock pile, when they were shooting at Dog" Claude, Sam, and Coop got out and looked around. Coop crawled over the fence and looked in the rocks. Sure enough there was the can Joey had opened. Claude and Coop walked back into the pasture a little way. There they found the pickup tracks and with a closer look found where Joey had hidden.

Claude looked farther around the trees and found the car tracks again. He followed them and there was a spot that looked like blood on the ground. If everything Joey said was true, someone had been shot, and he sure believed everything Joey had said.

Sam, Coop, and Joey left after lunch, and Joey was glad. He could hardly wait. Sam took Joey home and had to dry his own tears when he saw Sara, Bevi, and Joey. Everyone cried and hugged and laughed at the same time. Joey looked around and said, "Where's Rags?" Sam was dreading that question. "Well, Joey, those men shot Rags. We found him where they put you in the pickup." Joey's chin quivered, and tears came to his eyes. "They didn't need to do that. He was just a little dog."

Chapter 23

After several weeks, Sam drove up to Sara's house one morning. Joey and Sara were fixing the fence around the yard. "Good morning," Sara called. "What brings you out so early?" Sam got out of the car and went to meet them. "Well, I just wanted to let Joey know that those men have been picked up. We have all three in jail. That Sheriff Fleming too," Sam said. "I'm sure glad you got all of them," said Joey. "Sims would be glad to know that the four of them would never hurt anyone again." said Joey. "Four?" said Sam. "Did you say four?" "Yes, sir, there were four of them. Sims had it down in his book and I saw them." Sam thought for a minute. Then he said, "Joey, you may need to go back with me and tell me which one is missing." "Oh no," said Sara, "he isn't going anywhere." "Now, now Sara," said Sam, "he is the only one who has seen these people. He has to go and identify them." Sara's chin quivered, and tears welled up in her eyes. "Sam, please don't take him there again. I just don't think I can handle that." Sam knew Sara didn't want Joey out of her sight, and he couldn't blame her for that, but he really needed Joey to identify those men.

Sara turned away from Sam and said, "Come on in the house. I need some water. We'll talk about this." Sam smiled and followed her into the house. He could tell she had a lot on her mind. Joey and Bevi and Dog stayed outside on the porch. That dog had sure found a home with these kids, Sam thought.

Sara sat at the table and was very quiet. She seemed to only have bad news anymore. Sam saw a letter on the table from the U.S. Department of Army. His heart gave a little skip. What was that about, he wondered. Just as he was about to ask, Sara said, "Sam, I know you need Joey. I know you will bring him back. But, I have just had bad news about Carl. And I'm not sure I can take any more." She reached for a napkin and wiped her eyes.

"I haven't told the children yet," she said. "I'm not sure I can explain any of this to them." She reached for the letter and handed it to Sam. He read the short message and said, "Sara, I'm so sorry. But look, it says he is missing and it is assumed he is a prisoner. It does not say he is dead. There is hope and you must look at it that way. Missing means he may be alive"

Around the corner, Joey and Bevi stood listening. Joey's stomach ached. Dad was a prisoner? Where? Who had him? Bevi looked at Joey and tears welled up in her eyes. Sam saw them and got up and put his arms around both of them. "You have to believe your Dad is alright. Everyone thought you were gone for good, Joey, and you know it worked out. It will for your Dad too, if the Army can get to him."

Joey knew he had to be strong and not cry. He took a deep breath and said, "Mom, I have to go with Sheriff Sam. We need our cows back, and I know who took 'em. You know I'll be alright." Sara smiled, wiped her eyes and nodded her head. She knew he was right. She also knew he was growing up too fast.

Sam, Joey, and Dog left at noon. Joey knew he would be safe with Dog. They drove a long time and when they got to Ranger Miles' place, it was almost dark. Claude and Annie were glad to see him. Claude said arrangements had been made and Joey would be able to see a lineup the next morning and that no one would be able to see him.

Sam and Claude were up early. After everyone had eaten, Sam said it was time to go. Joey was a little nervous about doing something he had never done before. Dog got in the back of the pickup. Sam was amused that he was so protective of Joey.

When they arrived at the courthouse, there were lots of people and deputies everywhere. Sam, Joey and Dog followed Claude into a room on the second floor. He told Joey they were going into a small room and he would be shown some men and that if any of them were the ones that had held him prisoner, he was to tell him which one. "Can Dog come too?" asked Joey. Claude smiled and nodded okay. Sam waited outside in the larger room.

Joey, Dog, and Claude went inside and closed the door. All of a sudden there was a light at one side. Joey jumped. "It's alright" said Claude. "There they come now." Dog moved closer to Joey. He started that low growl. "It's okay, Dog," said Joey, "we are hid pretty good." "Do you recognize any of them Joey?" asked Claude. Joey looked real close. They had on clean clothes and they looked different but he knew who they were. "Yes, Sir, I do. That one on the end there is the one that shot Sims and the one next to him is the Sheriff that said he would take me home and didn't, and that one in the red shirt is the one they called Jake." Claude waited a little bit and then he said, "Is that all of them?" "No, sir, there was another one that come out and Sims said his name was Wesley. He ain't, ah I mean I don't see him there."

Claude remembered that Sims had written something in his notes like that. As well as he remembered, Sims said he wore fancy dress clothes like a lawyer. "Wait here, Joey, I'm going to see if there are any more for you to see. Okay?" said Claude. "Yes sir" said Joey. Claude left the room. Joey saw the men in the line up start to move off. He watched and then there was some more that came up. They were dressed like the preacher dressed. Claude came back in and said "do you see any here that looks like Wesley?" "No sir, I don't see him there."

Claude and Sam had to sign some papers and Joey had to put his name on one paper also. Sam said it was a statement saying those three men held him prisoner and that they had shot Sims and had kidnaped him when they stole the cows. After that, they went down to the bottom floor and started to go out the door when Dog started to growl and moved aganist Joey. Claude could not understand what the dog was doing. Joey took hold of Dog and looked around in the direction Dog was looking. There he was at the door of the elevator. "There he is," said Joey. "There goes the man named Wesley." "Where?" said Sam. "Which one?" "He just went in that door over there." said Joey. Claude started for the elevator with Sam right behind him. Sam had grabbed Joey by the arm. Dog took every step Joey took.

Sam and Claude watched the elevator. It didn't stop on the second floor, it went to the fourth floor. Claude pushed for the other elevator, the door opened, and when it closed, Claude pushed four. Claude was intent on catching the fourth man. "Joey, if you see this man again, I want you to catch hold of my hand. Do you understand?" Claude said. "Yes sir, but why?" He asked. "We don't have time for me to explain right now. Don't you talk though until I ask you to, alright?" Claude asked. "Yes sir" Joey said just as the elevator door opened.

The hall was empty and there was nothing but offices up here. Claude and Sam started down the hall with Joey and Dog right behind them. Claude was headed for an office where the door was open and a light was on. When he got there, he pushed the door open and said, "Hello" to the lady behind the desk. "Can you tell me whose office this is please?" The lady smiled and said, "this is Judge Black's office. This is his new office, and his name is not on the door yet. Could I help you find someone?" she said. "Well" said Claude, "we are looking for a man and the only name I have is Wesley." "Oh, yes, you mean Alan Wesley. His office is two doors down. I think the name on the door is JBF, Inc." she said. "Thanks." said Claude, "Ah, is the Judge in?" "Well, yes he is," she said. "I wonder if I could see him a second?" Claude asked. "Let me check with him," the lady said. Sam had moved out the door and was watching the second door down. Claude went into the Judge's office and in just a few minutes, they both came out.

Sam and the Judge shook hands and Claude introduced Joey also. They headed down the hall and knocked on the JBF, Inc. door. A man's voice called for them to come in. Dog growled. "Ssh, Dog," said Joey in a whisper. "You need to keep quite right now." Claude opened the door and there right before Joey eyes, was the man that Sims called Wesley.

The Judge said, "Alan, I have some folks I'd like for you to meet." Joey reached for Claude's hand. After some small talk, the Judge turned to Claude and said, "Do you have any questions of Mr. Wesley?" "Yes, I have," said Claude. "Do you know the Sheriff Fleming that was arrested for cattle rustling?" "Well, I can't say I know him personally. I had a call from someone that wanted me to be his lawyer at a trial, if it goes that far." Mr. Wesley said. "Why do you ask?" Claude turned to Joey, "Is this the man that was at the barn the night Bob hit Sims?" Claude asked. "Ye-Yes sir it is." replied Joey. Wesley looked shocked. "Why kid, what are you talking about? I've never seen you before in my life." he snapped. "What's that dog doing up here?" he said as he moved toward the door, but Claude and Sam stepped in front of him. "You are under arrest for cattle rustling, murder, kidnaping and anything else I can find on you" said Claude.

He reached for his handcuffs and the Judge patted Joey on the shoulder. "I've been following this case pretty close. I think I know now where you were kept. Was there a shack and a big barn with a loft?" he asked. "Yes, Sir, it was. It was a way back off the road I think." Joey said. "You are right about that and now that I see this sign I know where the place is." Turning to Claude he said, "It's the old JFB Ranch. Granny Fleming died several years back. Her grandson inherited the place. I'm sure glad she's not around to see how he turned out."

After a long wait, they all got into the Sheriff's car and the Judge rode with them and pointed the way. When they got to the place and got out, Joey recognized it alright. There was the barn and the metal water tank. "The license number is scratched on the board in the loft." said Joey. "What license number?" asked Sam. "The one on the pickup the Sheriff was driving the day Sims was hit." said Joey.

Dog was running everywhere sniffing the ground. The Judge went with Joey to see the license number. When they came down from the barn loft, Dog was digging at the place where the water tank was. Sam and Claude pulled and pulled on the tank and finally moved it out of the way. The ground was loose and Dog started digging again. Sam picked up a shovel and after a bit, there was Sims. Joey nearly got sick. The deputy went to the car radio and called for help. The Judge said all four men would be in prison for a long, long time.

The Judge looked at Joey and said, "Young man, you have been a very brave boy. Is there anything I can do for you?" Joey thought for a minute and then he said "Do you know Mr. and Mrs. Gray?" "I don't believe I do. Why?" "Oh, I just wanted to tell them thanks and that I really did get home." Joey looked around at the barn and the house and said, "Come on, Dog, let's go home."

About the Author

Emma Richardson Dudney, one of three children, was born in Eolian, Tx., a small community south of Breckenridge, Tx. Her first school was a one room school with all grade levels. She was seven years old when her father joined the navy during World War II. On his return, he purchased the family farm in Gunsight, Tx. Emma's greatest desire was to play the piano. At thirteen years of age, she was playing and singing with her father's gospel quartet. Today she and her husband live in Odessa, Tx. surrounded by a pistachio orchard. She enjoys teaching Sunday School, singing, playing her piano, and writing fiction stories for her children, grandchildren, and great grandchildren. Her desire when writing *Joey's Journey* was to capture suspense, adventure, love for family and clean literature for children eight to twelve years of age.

Printed in the United States
26154LVS00003B/172-330

9 781420 827057